HELL'S KITCHEN

Dear Kerri,
Hope you enjoy meeting
the Barbieri Boys!
love,
Catherine Hart

HART
SAINT
GERMAIN

HELL'S KITCHEN
Callie Hart & Lili Saint Germain
Copyright © 2015 Callie Hart & Lili Saint Germain

Formatted by Max Effect

FOR HE TODAY THAT
SHEDS HIS BLOOD WITH ME
SHALL BE MY BROTHER;
BE HE NE'ER SO VILE

–ST. CRISPIN'S DAY SPEECH
HENRY V, THE BARD.

PROLOGUE
ROBERTO

"FIND THAT LITTLE IRISH BITCH," I SAY, SURVEYING MY sons with disdain. Disdain is fast becoming the norm where Sal and Theo are concerned, but surely they're capable of doing this one thing for me. One thing that will show those Irish fuckers they can't screw with the Barbieri family and get away with it. One thing that will ensure the McLaughlins never fuck with us again.

As far as days go, it's a shitty day to kidnap someone, let alone the most protected bitch in the entire state of New York, but this ain't our first time at the rodeo. So long as the boys think with their heads and not their cocks, it should be a simple task.

"This air-conditioning sucks balls," Sal, my younger boy says. He's right, but his tone irritates me so much, I have to clench my fists to stop myself from retaliating with violence.

He's got nothing to complain about, standing there like a cocky little prick, watching me do the food prep. It's hot as fuck in Hell's Kitchen as it is, but standing next to the industrial deep fryer as I drop thin slices of veal into bubbling oil, it's positively sweltering.

"We got a starting point?" Sal asks.

The meat sizzles as it hits the burning fat. "Been a long time since I had to hold your fucking dick for you when you had to take a piss, son. You seem to be able to figure that out all on your own these days. I'm sure you can figure this out, too. How hard can picking up a teenage girl really be?"

Theo, shirtsleeves rolled up to his elbows, hands covered in blood—a picture of violence, as always—shrugs. "She's not just some kid we can snatch off the short bus. She's got bodyguards. Two of them. Ex-military bastards."

"One of them's a fucking woman," I spit. I cast my eyes over my sons: first Salvatore, then Theo, not sure who I'm more pissed off with. Not sure which one of them is the least like me. If I hadn't kept a close eye on my wife before she fucking died, there's a strong possibility I'd be questioning our boys' paternity. Fucking weak, both of them. Just like their mother.

"Hey," I snap, "you getting my meat ready or finger-fucking it over there?"

Sal snickers. Theo scowls.

"What the fuck are you laughing at, boy?" I hiss.

Sal shrugs as he pushes off the wall he's been leaning against and reaches into the waistband of his jeans, pulling out his Glock and checking the chamber. Seemingly satisfied, he tucks the gun back in place. "Got a photo?"

I make a small sound of irritation in the back of my throat as I pause my deep frying and wipe my hands on the rag that hangs over my shoulder. Reaching into my breast pocket, I pull out a 5x7 print and hand it over to my younger son. Sal pinches the photograph between his thumb and index finger and pulls, but I make no move to let go. "We've got one chance at this, you understand? You don't get her this time, we're fucked."

If only they knew.

Sal nods, and I finally let the photograph slip from my grasp. Theo, still elbow deep in meat and blood, cocks his head to the side, motioning for Sal to bring the photo closer. Sal obliges, standing beside his brother and holding the photograph up for both of them to see.

I can already anticipate the reaction these two will have. Kaitlin McLaughlin grew the fuck up. And she grew up hot. Long platinum blonde hair, arrow-straight. Green eyes, flecked with brown. Full lips, the works. She looks fuckable, but in a barely legal kind of way. I already know that Theo's pretty good at spotting girls under the age of consent, and this kid still has a look of jail time about her. A hint of arrogance, too. It lurks behind the cold smile that teases at the corners of her mouth—like she knows something you don't, only I do know her secrets. Nevertheless, girls like that are always trouble. Always better off avoided like the plague. And here I am, about to send these two after the kid like I've got a goddamn death wish. "How old?" Theo asks.

"Does it matter?" I don't look up from his task. I can feel

7

Theo's eyes on me, and I wonder if he's staring at the deep, purple scar that zigzags down my temple and over my cheekbone as I work. He has a hard time looking me in the eye, that one, too fascinated with my war wounds. "She's Paddy McLaughlin's blood," I say emphatically. "This is the way it's always been. The sins of the father are visited upon the heads of his children. She could be thirty or she could be three fucking months old. It wouldn't matter. We'd still be having this conversation. Paddy McLaughlin's people have fucked with *our* people. And now we're gonna fuck with his."

Sal baulks. "You want us to kill Paddy's *daughter?*"

I lift my head, lift my knife—and point the business end at my sons. "You two don't touch a single hair on her fucking head, you understand? That's above your pay grade." I stab the end of the knife into the chopping board in front of me. The wood splinters apart with the force of my rage. Reaching into my pocket, I pull out a folded piece of paper and slap it into Sal's open palm. "Program this number into your phone. Right now."

"What is it?" Strange numbers never normally equal anything good, and he knows this better than anyone by now. His fingers still quickly key the number into his cell as he frowns at me, though.

"I have something coming up. Something big that I need a professional to deal with. That number belongs to one of Charlie Holsan's ex employees."

"Charlie Holsan? The crazy English bastard that runs Seattle?" Theo asks.

"Charlie Holsan ain't running shit these days. Guy got

stabbed in the neck with a fork from what I hear. No one is running Seattle now, and I want that fucking city. A power vacuum needs to be filled, boys."

"And that's the big job?" Sal asks, screwing the paper into a ball and tossing it into the trash. "You want to take Seattle? Why not let us do it?"

I shake my head, pounding a tenderizing hammer into the meat on the chopping board in front of me. Why do they insist on knowing everything? "Kidnap the girl. Bring her back here. Call that number and get the motherfucker on side. *Today.* That's all you boys need to worry about. Now get to fucking work."

CHAPTER ONE
THEO

"WE'RE KIDNAPPING A TEENAGER. WE SHOULD BE wearing balaclavas and overalls, not fucking Armani suits." Tugging at the overly starched collar of my white shirt, I shrug my shoulders, trying to somehow make my clothes fit better. I haven't worn this suit since our mother died. Should have burned the fucking thing the same day. First thing I found when I put on the damn jacket this morning was the folded service program from St. Francis Xavier's Catholic Church in the breast pocket. That and a pack of six-year-old unsmoked cigarettes. Mom fucking hated me smoking. I'd wanted to light up so bad as they were lowering her coffin into the ground but all I could think about was her slapping me round the back of the head, giving me shit about my life choices. The girls I fucked. The crap I ate. The car I drove. The booze I drank. All of it. I was twenty-three back then and

I thought none of it mattered, that I was gonna live forever.

These days I'm far more aware of my own mortality. Knowing I'm liable to get shot in the head at any moment, just like my mother did, hasn't done much to alter the life choices she disapproved of so much. If anything, the knowledge has probably made them worse. I could die tomorrow. What's the point in living off salad and drinking fucking light beer when you could be getting your dick sucked and eating steak?

"She's not likely to climb into a town car with two guys she doesn't know if they're wearing ski masks, Theo. She's more likely to call her dad and have his boys come down to the airfield and pump our ride full of holes." Salvatore gives me a dry look. His left eyebrow nearly hits his hairline. "We should just execute the bitch on the runway and have done with it. Get her on her knees and then—" He forms the shape of a gun with his right hand, pulling back the action with his left, and then firing. "*Pcheeew.* Job done."

"No. No, job *not* done. Didn't you hear what Roberto said? He wants her safely delivered back to the house. Not one hair harmed, he said." It's been like this forever—Sal wanting to tear off half-cocked, completely disobeying our father, and me, grabbing him by the scruff of his neck and holding him back. "You're not executing anybody. Jesus Christ, Sal. The old man's unhinged, and we are *not* invincible. He's business down to the bone. If he needs to make an example out of us, he fucking will."

Sal doesn't say anything. He's very good at that—keeping his mouth shut when he disagrees with something that's being said. He holds onto it for days, months, years and then dredges it up, verbatim, whenever it suits him. Usually when he wants to demonstrate that you're being an asshole or contradicting yourself in some way.

He holds up his cell phone and waves it in my peripherals. "If you don't want to piss off our father, we should call that fucking specialist, right? The Seattle guy?"

Anger spikes through me. However, the emotion isn't as intense as it could be, given our father's distrust. We've met the specialist Roberto mentioned, and he's one scary mother-fucker. Straight up and down, though. No fucking around. He's not a bad guy to have on your side. I sure as shit wouldn't want him on anyone else's. I grunt my ascent, fixing my eyes on the road. "Fine. Do it. Get it out of the way."

Sal hits the number saved in his phone and we both sit there, stewing over the injustice of having to answer to some outsider. Or ask for his advice. I know my brother, too. This is a particularly bitter pill for him to swallow.

He hits speakerphone, and the line rings six times before someone eventually picks up. There's no voice, though. No one says anything. Sal looks at me, pissed off, rolls his eyes, and then speaks into the receiver. "What's up, asshole. Roberto Barbieri asked us to call you."

"Roberto Barbieri shouldn't even have this number," someone growls on the other end of the line. The guy's voice is pretty much the sound of an earthquake. Of rock grinding on rock. I remember that about him—that his voice alone was enough to make people shit their pants. I take the phone away from Sal and speak into it quickly, before Sal gets the chance.

"Mr. Mayfair, we met back in Seattle a couple of months ago. I believe we had a common enemy. The Monterellis? You took care of one brother? We took care of the other?"

The Monterellis had always been cocky motherfuckers. When Frankie got shot in the face by this Mayfair guy for fucking up some skin trade deal, the younger brother, Archie, had risen up the food chain and started overstepping boundaries that had been in place for years. The Monterellis don't run gambling on the east coast. They don't deal with the Russians anywhere in the USA. The Russians are ours, especially if they want drugs or guns or women. The only thing that should have been buying from the small time west coast Italians was fucking vegetables.

Roberto sent us over to Seattle to deal with the problem, and once again Sal had gone off half cocked. He'd shot the guy three times in the chest but hadn't actually killed the fucker. We'd had to break into a hospital of all places to finish the job: Colombian necktie this time, just like our father would have wanted. Colombian neckties are his speciality. His cut throat razor has actually cut more throats than I can count.

"I remember," the guy on the other end of the line answers. "The cops pinned me for that one, too. Made life very difficult for me and my girl."

"We're sorry about that. The method of execution's usually enough to tip the cops off over here in New York." It shocked me the first time I saw someone having their throat cut—just how violent the force of the gushing blood could be. When Sal had laid the steel against Monterelli's skin, the spray of

13

blood had literally hit the ceiling.

"Seattle cops don't know shit about Roberto Barbieri. And they don't care, either. You guys made a mess."

Sal bristles, reaching for the phone, but I won't let him have it. "Irrespective of what happened, Roberto wants to hire you. He's offering big money for you to fly out to New York."

"I don't work for other people, *Theo*," Mayfair says. He knows my name, which is pretty typical. He's the kind of guy who will know everything about me, the same way he knows everything about every single member of organized crime syndicates in America, just so he has the drop on everyone. No surprises that way.

"You'd be a contractor. My father would give you free rein to handle the job however you pleased. You'd be here for a couple of days, do the work and then you'd be flying home again. Simple."

"The kind of jobs your father hires men like me for are never simple. I'm west coast these days, Theo. And I don't kill people for money anymore. Tell your father thanks but no thanks. Don't call this number again."

The line goes dead. I can feel Sal's eyes searing into the side of my head, burning into me. "Well, that went well," he says, his voice flat. "At least the old bastard can't say we didn't do as we were told."

It occurs to me that our father told us to get the motherfucker on side, not call him and have him tell us no. That's semantics, though. I'll worry about Mayfair and Roberto's massive score later, after we've dealt with this girl and gotten the old man's birthday celebrations out of the way tonight.

I shift up a gear, swerving the innocuous Lincoln town car I'm driving through a maze of yellow taxicabs and other Lincoln town cars. This is how everyone travels in the city. If you have money, you don't take the subway. You don't ride the bus. You have a driver and a sleek five-door sedan that will take you anywhere you want to go.

That's what Kaitlin McLaughlin is expecting to collect her from the MacKinnon Commercial Airfield, an hour's drive out of New York Proper: a nameless driver, who will transport her back to her father's bar in Hell's Kitchen.

Instead, she's getting my brother and me: two very pissed-off Italian boys, both with severe attitude problems and a distinct dislike for anything even faintly Irish. You can't really escape hating the people your father hates, especially when your father is Roberto Barbieri. The guy's not just old school. He has a medieval mentality and can hold a fucking grudge like no one else on earth. You piss him off and you can expect some serious Old Testament justice: an eye for an eye, motherfucker. And that's you getting off light.

"What time they due to land?" Sal asks. He loops a tie, pre-knotted and ready to go, over his head.

"Twenty minutes." With traffic the way it is, we'll be there in ten.

Sal tightens the tie around his neck, placing the ridiculous fucking chauffeur's hat on his head. He tucks his hair back behind his ears. He needs to cut it, but will the bastard listen? Hell, no. He never listens to a word I say. "Are you ready?" he asks.

I take my eyes off the road, arching an eyebrow at him. Who the hell does he think he's talking to? I've been doing this job longer than him, after all. I've never blinked. Never *not* been ready. He gets the point pretty damn quickly.

"All right, man, I'm sorry."

When we arrive at the airfield, we're directed to hangar twelve, no questions asked. Paddy McLaughlin's own men would have arrived around now—if we hadn't already beaten the shit out of them and handcuffed them to a pillar inside an old cardboard factory down on the wharf—so we're expected. Kaitlin McLaughlin's plane is delayed. I'm already bored and itching to go by the time the private jet touches down. Sal climbs out of the car and leans against the front passenger door, waiting for the prissy Irish princess and her entourage to exit the plane. When she does, we're in luck.

Normally, Paddy doesn't send his little girl anywhere without two personal bodyguards. Today, she's only accompanied by one. Sal taps the hood of the car as he goes out to take her bags. I have the engine purring in anticipation as he opens the back passenger side door for her and she climbs inside.

Huge sunglasses cover her eyes. That full mouth of hers is perfectly visible in the rearview, though. "Where the fuck is Ray?" she asks. Her father may be first generation Irish, but Kaitlin was born and raised in the States—she sounds like a spoiled little Yank bitch.

"Mr. McLaughlin needed him for something else. He sent us instead."

She slides the sunglasses down the bridge of her nose,

peering at me over the car's half-raised privacy screen. "And who are you?"

I give her a tight-lipped smile, doing my best to keep my tongue in my head. We need the bodyguard to get in the car, and then we're golden. Until then, I'm Jerry, the friendly town car driver. "Jerry. My buddy there, that's Gareth. We're new."

"I can see that." She makes a low, humming sound at the back of her throat. She sounds like she approves. *Sorry, sweetheart. I don't touch crazy pussy. But I* will *introduce you to my old man, all the same. He just can't wait to fucking meet* you.

The door behind me opens and I feel the car dip as someone gets in—I didn't notice before, but the lone bodyguard with Kaitlin is a woman. Must be the chick Roberto was talking about. I get a good look at her in the rearview and find myself taking a second one for good measure. She's blisteringly hot. Maybe in her mid-twenties? Long dark hair, tied back into a braid. High cheekbones. A mouth to rival Kaitlin's. Her tits strain against her tight black shirt as she twists to put on her seatbelt. You can tell she works out; her clothes fit her far too well for her not to know she looks good in them, too.

Just like Kaitlin, she asks, "Where's Ray?"

"Busy doing something for Daddy," Kaitlin informs her, which saves me from spinning the lie again.

"Okay. Straight to the bar, then." The body guard's head doesn't even lift, but she's a professional. She assesses me in the mirror just as I've assessed her. I pretend not to notice as Sal folds himself into the passenger seat.

17

"Of course." I press the button for the privacy screen, raising it the rest of the way, blocking out all sound from the back of the car. Sal turns and gives me one of his wicked, crazy-ass grins. He's enjoying this already. "All right, then, big brother. Let's do this." He leans forward and hits a button on the dash—and every single door on the town car automatically locks. "No backing out now."

I burn out of the hangar to the sounds of muffled thuds from the back of the car. The bodyguard's not stupid. She's heard the doors locking and knows something isn't right. *"Motherfucker! Open this up right now!"*

Normally there's an intercom in these cars, but this one's different. Sal and I smashed the shit out of *this* car's intercom with two lump hammers and ripped out the wiring. We also lined the roof with lead. The girls in the back aren't striking up a conversation with us any time soon. And they aren't making any phone calls to dear old Papa McLaughlin, either.

As I head back toward the city, the shouting from the back gets louder. It's accompanied by the dull thudding of feet trying to smash out the privacy screen. Sal raps his knuckles against the glass, grinning again. "Bitch sounds crazy back there. I don't think she likes the modifications we've made."

I allow myself a small smile as we hit the George Washington Bridge, heading back toward North Manhattan. So far *Operation: Kidnap Kaitlin* has been a roaring success. Sal pulls out his cell and starts tapping into it with quick fingers. "Telling the old man we're on our way?"

He nods. "Bastard better give us credit where credit's due. He's probably still organising his own fucking birthday party.

Meanwhile, *we* have just successfully taken our mark hostage. We're on the homeward stretch."

The fucking homeward stretch.

The thing about saying you're on the homeward stretch is that often it's like waving a red flag at a bull. Fate must hear that phrase and decide to fuck over the poor schmuck who was dumb enough to utter it every single fucking time. It's only seconds after Sal's parted with those words that the electric window behind me—the bodyguard's side window— shatters. We knew the bodyguard would be armed, but we didn't expect anyone to be shooting out the damn *side* windows. An eruption of fragmented diamonds explodes sideways, spraying a bright yellow smart car with a million shards of glass. The sound of the firing gun is almost deafening.

"*What the fuck?*"

The smart car veers sideways, smashing into us; I press my foot to the floor, grinding my teeth at the sound of screeching metal and more hammering from the back as I swerve through the traffic. Sal twists in his seat, pulling his gun and pressing it to the glass of the privacy screen. His finger's on the trigger. "She's going fucking crazy. I'm gonna shoot the bitch."

"Which one?"

Sal lifts one shoulder, scowling into the back. "I don't know. Both of them. I need to shoot both of them."

I careen over in the left hand lane, trying to find a clear path. We need to get back to the fucking restaurant. *Now.* This is really not fucking good. Risking a glance in the mirror behind me, I see my brother is right. Kaitlin appears to be crying, thick black streaks of makeup running down her face, her arrogance completely gone now. The bodyguard, on the other hand, is only half visible. She's ... *she's leaning out of the fucking window.* I glance in the side mirror just in time to see her aiming her gun. She fires. The side mirror reports the muzzle flash, and then the whole thing is just ... *gone.*

"Fuck!"

"That's it. I'm shooting them."

"DO NOT FUCKING SHOOT ANYONE, SAL!" If I can't pull this car over or get the hell out of this traffic, my brother is gonna get trigger happy on these bitches and we'll be carting two bodies back into our father's kitchen. Sal gives me a frustrated look, his eyebrows spiking. A look of surprise washes over him.

"She's gonna fucking shoot—" He doesn't get to finish the sentence. An ear-splitting *crack* rips through the air. Suddenly glass is raining down on me. Glass everywhere. The bitch in the back fires a second shot; this time the round travels straight through my broken window and shatters the windshield from the inside.

I can't see a fucking thing.

Kaitlin starts screaming even louder.

I don't have the car anymore. I don't have this situation. I don't have my fucking brother, either. I think he's about to murder our collateral. My thoughts as the car hits the guardrail, as the car begins to flip: *We'd better just fucking die. Because if we don't fucking die ... what the* fuck *are we gonna tell Roberto?*

CHAPTER TWO
SCARLETT

I STARE AT THE BROKEN AIR-CONDITIONING UNIT IN my tiny walk-up—a room that's really just a broom cupboard with a refrigerator and a mattress—and sigh inwardly. It's easily ninety degrees outside, and it's only eight-fifteen in the morning. New York City is excruciating on days like this, days and weeks that melt into each other, a constant barrage of humidity and steam and loose wisps of hair that stick to the back of your neck. It's hotter than hell in this damn city, and all I want to do is *get out*. The problem is, to get out you kind of need somewhere to go.

The air conditioner hasn't worked since I've had the place—seven months now, seven months since I've been ousted from L.A. Seven months. How is that even possible? It feels like it happened yesterday, the image of his little tricycle rolling backwards behind the car the same thing that haunts me in my nightmares. Seven months since I took a plea deal, a suspended sentence. Which means it's been—I have to stop and count back. Nine? Yeah. Nine months since the night when I completely ruined my fucking life and ended someone else's.

As I slam my door and take the nine flights of stairs down to the lobby, I realize roughly halfway down that I didn't even try the elevator to see if it's working yet. For three weeks, I've been hauling my ass up and down these stairs, because the building super refuses to do anything about it. And it's not like I'm about to knock on his door and ask again after the way he creeped me the fuck out last week, standing in his doorway and not letting me out of his apartment for almost an hour. Jimmy. You know what? I've never met a Jimmy who wasn't a dick, now that I think about it. This one is a total creeper, though. The guy is a date rape waiting to happen.

Thick, muggy air hits me square in the face as I leave my building, sucking the air out of my lungs as my feet hit the sidewalk. I'm still not used to this damp, oppressive kind of heat after growing up on the west coast, still forget to ready myself for the onslaught every time I go outside in this goddamn city since summer has begun.

I cross the street, threading my way through the cabs and town cars that choke the city at this hour. As I pass over a subway grate, a thick billow of steam blasts up into the street. It's forceful enough that I cough on the acrid air as it forces into my lungs and coats my face with a filmy residue.

Motherfucker! My makeup is probably ruined, and I'm already running late. I don't have time to run back up nine flights and reapply, so I keep walking. It doesn't matter what I look like anymore, so why do I care?

I don't look at anyone as I walk to the diner. I keep my face down, my eyes skimming the sidewalk and the crowd just ahead, only enough to make sure I don't collide with anyone. They don't like that here. In New York, you walk in a straight fucking line and you stay out of everyone's way. I'm maybe three blocks from my work when I hear it: a high-pitched scream from a child, a car braking so hard its tires squeal in protest. I can't help it. My knees turn to liquid and I'm in serious danger of passing the fuck out and being trampled to death.

It's bizarre, the way sounds affect me these days. The way most things affect me. The inconsequential things that other people don't even register are the same things that set terror alight in my heart. You know, the way dogs howl at sirens and cower, terrified, when they hear thunder. That's me with *everything*.

I just need to get to work. I'll get to work, swallow one of my little white pills, and I'll be golden. Three blocks. Three blocks. Three blocks.

I don't want to turn my eyes toward the scream but I can't help it; it's like my mind revels in my frightened state, my awkward inability to block out the simplest of things. I might be a person nobody knows, a girl with my face turned down to the pavement so nobody sees me, but I see them. I see all of them. I hear them.

And it hurts.

My eyes scan the ever-moving sea of people in front of me,

everybody with their own purpose. Me, I feel like I'm just floating along from one day to the next, eating and working and sleeping and trying to stop the weight of my sins from pulling me under. People say drowning is a peaceful way to die. But I've been drowning for nine months, and I can tell you, there's nothing peaceful about clawing at the air in front of you every time you wake up in the morning, unable to breathe, trying to stay afloat.

I finally find the source of the screaming: a boy with a mop of blond hair, thick and shaggy, but cut blunt all around the bottom. I imagine his mother placing a bowl on his head as he wriggles on a stool, taking great pains to cut the hair that hangs in his eyes without accidentally cutting her antsy child.

I can only see him in profile, but he's turning toward me, and I know if he does I'll see the color of his eyes. *Don't be blue.* My own eyes don't work quickly enough, can't swivel to the side before he's facing me, still screaming, blood on his knee. *They're fucking blue.*

He fell over on the sidewalk and scraped his knee. Of course. He didn't get hit by a car. He didn't go underneath the tires with a sickening thud. He needs a Band-Aid, and I need to chill the fuck out. The relief that floods my limbs almost dizzies me. He's not going to die. *He's not going to die.*

My cell phone beeps loudly, making me jump. I reach into my handbag, seeing a text from my cousin Elliot. I swipe the screen and read his message.

ELLIOT: Hey Scar. Got some friends

who need a place to crash tonight.
You know the drill. Is your place free?

I fight the urge to roll my eyes. The last thing I want is someone crashing in my tiny walk-up, but it wouldn't be the first time it's happened. I owe Elliot big time after he helped with the court case. Without him, I'd be rotting in a jail cell somewhere. I slow my pace so I can tap a reply message into the screen.

ME: Sure thing. I'm off work at six.
There's a spare key in the plant next
to my door if they arrive earlier.

I lock the phone and drop it into my bag, irritated that I won't be alone tonight. It's a lot harder to get drunk with strangers in the room. Which makes me think—I need a drink. The Victoria's Secret perfume bottle in my bag weighs heavy on my shoulder, full of vodka instead of flowery scent— just a fifth, because I'm supposed to be stone-cold sober as part of my parole conditions—and my mouth practically waters at the thought of locking myself away in the bathroom and having just a little sip to make the day slightly less shitty. Booze and pills, the things that get me through the days, until I decide I don't want to get through them anymore and jump off this express train through hell.

The diner is already busy when I arrive, morose and with the image of two little boys with blond hair and blue eyes stuck firmly in the front of my mind. One from this morning, and the other from nine months ago. It strikes me as strange that the *sound* of a kid's voice sets me off. The boy nine months ago didn't scream; I never even heard his voice. I saw him on the news once after I'd been arrested. It was a home video the reporters had somehow gotten their hands on when the media frenzy was at its peak. He liked Spiderman. He had this excited little voice when he spoke, a rasp in his throat, the tail end of a cold. In the video, he was showing his dad how he could climb a tree.

His name was Ryder. He was five years old, and then he was dead.

"You're late, Scarlett," Sylvia hisses as I pour coffee and take a sip, burning the entire roof of my mouth. My throat protests as the bitter liquid scalds on its way down, settling uneasily in my stomach where it will churn until Serge hands me a plate of leftovers and tries to slap my ass around ten-thirty, when the breakfast crowd slows.

Sylvia's a bitch. I know she steals my tips when I'm with other customers. For some reason, I'm the highest-tipped waitress in Cabrezzi's. Something about my shiny white teeth and my convincing smile? Or maybe it's because they feel like they know me, like I'm familiar, a washed-out, slightly chubbier version of the actress who used to appear on their TV screens every Tuesday night and save the world. It's the only reason she doesn't fire my ass. Italian Sylvia owns the place with her Russian husband, Serge, and together they're the oddest couple I've ever met. She wears the pants, bossing everyone around as she taps her taloned fingernails on her chipped coffee cup that says Cabrezzi's down the side, black letters on a yellowed white mug. She talks a mile a minute, makes me serve her family every time they come in, even though I'm the only waitress who doesn't speak Italian. And they don't tip. Like, at all. And Serge, her husband, fifty, with a paunch and a hint of his Russian accent still lingering on after thirty years in the Big Apple. He cooks greasy breakfast plates for the hungry hordes and tries to shove his hand in my dress whenever I have the misfortune to pass through the kitchen.

I choke a little, put the coffee down on the pass, and try to compose myself. In the first few months that I was here, I used to get angry when she spoke to me like this. Now, I barely even notice.

I pull my long brown hair up into a messy bun, the ends crunchy and dry as they slide through my fingers. I used to visit this hairdresser on Rodeo Drive every four weeks when I was back in LA, get my roots done and my ends trimmed, conditioning treatments, the works. I was sad in the beginning, after I'd lost everything, after all the money was gone and the best I could do was a package of dye from the supermarket that promised chocolate brunette but delivered dull black strands that looked oily all the time. Since then, I've barely bothered. The black has mostly faded. I don't even care anymore. When you've already lost everything, you eventually get to this weird place where you've got nothing left to lose, and no good reason to try and get anything better. I guess that's why I'm here, slinging coffees and waiting tables with my split ends and the ten pounds I've gained since my agent stopped passing me coke to help me starve myself. The camera adds ten pounds, they'd all said, but there were no cameras pointed at me anymore. Coke's an expensive habit, and I'm a poor bitch these days. I drink vodka, and I take as many Oxycontin pills as I can afford. It's better than fastening bricks to my feet and throwing myself in the Hudson. I think.

The first twenty minutes of my shift are predictably dull. The place gets busy. I smile until my face hurts, pocket my tips, duck off to the bathroom for a shot of the good stuff, keep my eagle eyes on both Sylvia's sticky fingers and the fingers Serge wishes he could get sticky in my pants, and then *shit. Gets. Interesting.*

The girl runs in first. Or rather, she bursts in, all wild blonde hair and too-large sunglasses. She rips the glasses off her face, her pale green eyes wild as she scans the diner. She's pretty, at least conventionally. She looks young, but like she's already had some work. I can spot it a mile off. Nose job? Definite. Lips? Filled with collagen to the hilt. I'm still not sure about her eyelids.

When she bursts in, I just happen to be the closest to the register up front. I've just started to feel a pleasant buzz from the vodka I drank in the bathroom, and her sudden entrance crashes right through the dulled edges of my morning.

"Can I help you?" I ask, irritated by her for some reason I can't put my finger on.

And then she starts to cry. Jesus Christ, I do not need a crying girl today. "I'm being chased," she whimpers, fat tears sliding down her face.

"Chased?" I'm so far unaffected. This is New York City; I've seen my fair share of crazy.

"Please," she says, stepping closer to me, and it's then I notice the bits of glass in her blonde hair. Her hand's bleeding, too. *Shit.* My concern kicks in, better late than never, as I study the rest of her. Torn shirt. Cuts and scratches on her face and arms, her knee purplish and bloated below her skirt. I return my gaze to her face. Her lips have seen some work, but the top one is swelling even bigger, the part below her nostrils turning a nice shade of yellowy-blue in front of my eyes.

"I'll call the police," I say, turning to grab the phone from next to the register. Before I can, a wet hand clamps down on my wrist and tugs forcefully. I turn back, suddenly pissed. I hate it when people touch me. Ever since that night, I can't stand it when people fucking touch me. The blonde must see the look on my face, because she drops my wrist like it's made of lead. I bring it up in front of me, finding a nice smear of her blood around my wrist. I'm both worried and revolted at once; this chick could have hepatitis or worse, and she's gone and bled on my fucking arm.

"I'm sorry," she says, looking over her shoulder. "Please, these guys have guns. These guys are going to kill me! Don't you have a back exit or something I could just sneak out of?"

A thrill shoots down my stomach before landing unpleasantly in my gut, where it churns away, mixing together with the bitter coffee and vodka I just drank, cheap caffeine and alcohol and fear bubbling through my veins. Suddenly, I want to be sick.

I look around the diner uneasily. What do I do? Do I help this girl? Is she telling the truth? I can't handle this shit so early in the morning.

I need another drink. Or a pill. Or both.

"Come with me," I say finally, taking her elbow and pulling her toward the ladies' room. She follows obediently, struggling to keep up as I march toward the bathroom and shove the door open.

"In here," I say. She hesitates for a moment, scanning my face, and I realize she probably thinks the toilets don't have an escape path.

"There's a fire escape in here," I say, tugging her arm again. "You want me to lose my job or what? Hurry up."

She follows me into the bathroom, and once she's safely inside I lock the door behind us. The fluorescent lights cast a sickly pallor over both of us—yet somehow, this girl still looks amazing, and I still look like I've been chewed up and spat out. Lovely.

"Fire escape," I say, pointing past three toilet stalls to a large steel door. These buildings in New York have the weirdest shit. Like, why anyone would have a fire escape in a women's bathroom beats me. Still, when I used to smoke, it became a well-loved refuge of mine in between taking orders and dodging Serge and Sylvia.

The chick pushes on the door, but it doesn't budge. She looks at me, and the panic on her face is almost comical.

"The key," I say dryly, reaching up to a windowsill and sliding a dust-covered key from its hiding spot. I unlock the door and push it open, gesturing for her to go inside.

"Oh, God, I thought you were one of them," she babbles as she steps slowly through the door. *Faster*, I think, pushing her gently through the doorway. I'm suddenly less worried and more irritated again. I need her to get the fuck out before Sylvia fires me for disappearing in the middle of breakfast service.

"What's your name?" I ask her, as she shrinks into the fire escape.

"Kaitlin," she says. "Kaitlin McLaughlin."

And then I know she's telling the truth.

I hear shouting in the diner, heavy footsteps. Kaitlin's eyes grow wide and glassy again. On impulse, I take my apartment key from my apron and press it into her palm. Reciting the address to her, I give rough directions and make her repeat them to me.

"Keep your head down," I instruct her, having no fucking idea what I'm about to get into. I don't want to get involved with the Irish. But I also don't want this girl to get shot while I watch. I've already got enough blood on my hands. "Go there and wait. I'll come help you."

The footsteps are getting closer. Shit! Someone's kicking the bathroom door. It splinters easily, flimsy piece of shit.

Kaitlin nods gratefully. I give her one last look before closing the fire escape door, locking it with the key. *She didn't even say thank you*, I think, as adrenaline spikes in my gut. I hurry over to the closest toilet stall as the bathroom door explodes off its hinges. I don't have time to look, though. I drop the key into the toilet bowl with a *plink* and reach for the flusher. At the same time, footsteps rain down on the tiles like bullets as a blur passes by the open toilet stall I'm crammed into. Someone throws themselves at the locked fire escape door, using their body weight to try and open it and failing miserably. The door is made of steel. Even Ironman isn't breaking that shit down.

I shrink deeper into the stall as the person stumbles back from the door and into my line of sight. I don't want to look. I don't want to know.

"Hey!" a deep voice yells. Instinctively, I look toward the source of the noise, both terrified and unreasonably calm, my fingers closing around the flush handle. The guy in front of me is scarily impressive, at least six four and pointing a gun in my face. Right in my face. I'm crammed in this stall, tucked on one side of the toilet, my hands itching. It feels like this is a dream. But it's not a dream. This is really happening.

"Don't do it," the guy warns.

I start to push the flusher down when he steps closer, glancing down at the lone silver-colored key in the toilet bowl. "I said *don't do it*. I need that key."

"Maybe you should ask nicely," I say, stalling. I hope the girl is far, far away by now, hauling ass to my apartment. I really don't want to watch her head explode if this guy catches up to her and plants a bullet in her head.

Then again, I also don't want to experience my own head exploding if he shoots *me*.

The guy, who looks more than slightly unhinged, cocks his head to the side and gives me a lopsided grin. "You look like a girl who does what she's told," he says, shaggy brown hair slipping over one hazel-colored eye.

"And you look like you should be driving a limo," I reply, looking pointedly at the ridiculous hat he's wearing. "So I guess we're both a lousy judge of character."

He sighs, shaking his head. "Okay, for you, I'll ask. Pretty fucking please, get your fucking hand off that fucking toilet so I can get that fucking key!"

He scowls at me, his mouth twitching as if he's incredibly angry.

I wonder if he'll shoot me. I wonder why I'm so calm.

I flush the key.

And then, all I see is his fist flying at my face. I suck in a breath, expecting to fall like a sack of potatoes, hoping I won't land face first in the toilet bowl and drown in three inches of rusty water. It'd be just my luck to die that stupidly. But his fist never reaches my face. Instead, it smashes into the veneer beside me that separates the stalls, the force so great that the wood splinters.

"You just made a big fucking mistake," he grinds out, his eyes suddenly millimetres from mine. He grabs my upper arm roughly. "You're gonna regret helping that little bitch, I guarantee you."

He looks around, disgusted, and I have to suppress the urge to giggle. Nope, too late. The high-pitched sound slips out of my mouth for a second, until I clamp my hand over my lips, cutting it off. What the hell is wrong with me? I shouldn't be giggling. This guy is scary as shit, he's got a gun, and he's pissed.

"What's so fucking funny?" he grunts, letting my arm drop and grabbing a chunk of my hair instead. I yelp, expecting pain, but all he does is snatch a bobby pin out of the bird's nest I styled so carefully this morning.

He unfolds the bobby pin and steps away from me, pressing one of the ends into the fire escape lock, giving it a jiggle. I slide sideways out of the toilet cubicle and back up a little, very slowly, thinking I can slip away while he's concentrating on trying to get the door open. I'm starting to regret helping this Kaitlin chick escape, because if Miss Irish Royalty is being chased, it's got to be some of the baddest motherfuckers in this city who would dare to pursue her. This guy's got to be with the Italians. A hitman, maybe? But why?

I'm starting to think I might actually be able to sneak out of here when a hand darts out and yanks me back toward the heavy door. "I can see what you're doing," he says, obviously unimpressed. I want to roll my eyes, but I'm too scared right now to do anything except stand mutely and try not to think about the way a bullet would tear my face in half. I feel like I'm going to pee my pants. And throw up. And cry.

"What are you doing?" I ask, as the guy releases my arm and resumes his work on the lock. "It's one of those magnetic locks," I add. "It needs the original key to unlock it."

The guy takes that in, presses his forehead to the door for a moment as he sighs loudly. "Fuuuuuuuuuuck," he groans, throwing the bobby pin on the ground near our feet. This entire time, he hasn't lowered his gun, like he's expecting me to attack him or something.

I hear sirens close by, and I know he does, too. He glances in the direction of the closed bathroom door. "Fuck," he mutters. "I don't want to hurt you, but—"

"So don't," I interrupt.

"I don't want to hurt you," he repeats, frowning, "but you've just lost my mark. You've ruined my entire fucking day."

I raise my eyebrows. "You're the one who lost her," I bite back. "All I did was help her get to safety." As soon as the words have left my mouth, I'm cursing myself. What the hell did I just say that for?

This guy, this *fucking* guy, turns from pissed off to amused as if I've just clicked my fingers and made it happen. His crooked smile returns as he licks his lips, the sirens almost on the diner's doorstep now.

"To *safety*, huh? And where exactly would that be?"

Holy Mother of God, I'm in deep shit.

CHAPTER THREE
GRACIE

WE'RE ON THE ROOF.

The passenger door yawns open, and Kaitlin is long gone. The silly bitch just sat there crying, chest heaving, while I sawed at her jammed seatbelt with one of my throwing knives, barely able to reach the webbing from where I was pinned. I could hear those two fuckheads up front, trying to wrestle themselves free, so I didn't have much time to shout at her. I had just about enough time to slap her across the face and tell her to run before the sound of groaning, twisted metal reached me—they were breaking loose. Then Kaitlin was scrambling out of the shattered window beside her, and she was skidding on broken glass and doing as I told her: *running*.

Five seconds have passed since then, and so far I'm still pinned on my side of the car. But I'm working on it. There's more breaking glass, and then the guy who came to escort us from the plane, the one with the long hair, is crouched down beside the window Kaitlin crawled through, staring straight at me. He has a gun in his hand. "Fuck!" he shouts. He doesn't seem impressed that Kaitlin's gone. Lifting the gun and aiming it right at me, he loses the safety. "Which way did she go?" he snaps.

I lift my own gun and I shoot. The round should hit him right in the face, but he's quick, I'll give him that. He ducks to the left, using the warped frame of the car as a shield. "Mother*fucker!*" he shouts.

"Quit wasting time!" the other one hollers from the driver's seat. "She went left. Get after her, man!"

I don't see the guy with the long hair again. I hear him swear, and then the sound of glass crunching under his shoes as he bolts after Kaitlin. She has a clear minute on him now, though. Hopefully that's enough. Do I care if the spoilt brat dies? Fuck no. She deserves it, I'm sure, but her father, my boss, will be less than happy if I allow her to end up with a bullet between her eyes. And I don't like displeasing my employer.

"You comfortable back there?" the guy in the front yells. I can just about hear him through the privacy screen, which has somehow not shattered. He and I must be in pretty much the same situation. His chair has driven back, pinning me in place, which probably means something has driven through the front of the car, pinning him, too.

"I'm just grand," I shout. "You'll forgive me if I don't stick around, though." I can see how I'm going to get out of this mess. I need to twist my body through the narrow gap between where I'm sitting and where Kaitlin was sitting. Problem is, the car's compressed in such a way that I have to pivot to slide myself through, and to do that I'm gonna need to dislocate my shoulder. Won't be the first time it's happened, which means it'll be slightly easier to accomplish, but it's still going to hurt like a fucker.

"Why don't you just stay put, sweetheart? I'd like to have a word, if that's all right with you?" the guy in the front shouts. I can hear the sarcasm dripping from his voice, combined with the same frustration I'm experiencing right now.

"I guess we'll just have to see who gets out of here first, huh?" I can't waste anymore time. I doubt this guy actually does want to talk to me. He's probably going to run after his friend, but not before executing me, if only to make sure I can't describe him to the boss. I take a deep breath and begin twisting my body. I manage to slide one arm through the gap and then my head, and then I've reached the point where I can't go any further. How do you prepare yourself for the pain of a dislocated shoulder? Short answer is, you don't. Especially if you know what's coming. You take a deep fucking breath, close your eyes tight, and you either do it or you don't.

I'm a doer. Or more appropriately, I'm a stubborn bitch and I won't let these two bastards get the better of me. A scream rips from my vocal chords as I pop my joint out of place. The pain is worse than I remember—I think for a second I'm going to throw up—but I don't have time to stop. If I hesitate, that means he wins. I'm now able to wriggle through the gap, so I kick and scramble my way through until

I can heave myself one-handed out of the window. On my back, staring up at the sky, I rotate my arm, take another deep breath and I yank my shoulder back into place.

I might as well have torn the damn thing off. I hiss out a curse word that would make a hardened criminal blush. I'm nearly blind with pain, but it's time to get up. Time to move. Time to get the hell away from this car. There are people on the bridge, watching on anxiously. Groups of men and women, standing well back, no one rushing forward to help. That's undoubtedly got something to do with the gun in my hand. Or the gun the long-haired guy was holding before he went charging off after Kaitlin. They all must have heard the shot I fired at him, too.

A tall, blonde woman, fingers pressed to her mouth, looks like she's about to step forward, but then she steps back instead, horror washing over her face. I know why. It's because that motherfucker's climbed out of the car and is standing right behind me. Must be.

I don't waste time looking. I push myself to my feet, spinning around, raising my gun. He's standing right behind me, a smug look on his blood-covered face. "You feel like having that chat now, sweetheart?" He smirks, as though he has the upper hand here, even though he isn't holding a weapon.

I know his type. The type who think female bodyguards exist so they can hand over tampons and keep their ward entertained by gossiping about boys. This guy's about to find out the hard way that I'm a little different. Cocking my gun, I aim for his right eye. "You can either turn around and hold up your hands, or I can create a sixth hole in your head, asshole. Up to you."

He looks away, laughing under his breath. The idea of me shooting him seems to be really fucking funny. "You're gonna shoot me? Here? In front of all these people?"

"You think I'm worried about getting busted by the cops? I'm not." As if on cue, sirens begin to wail in the distance. It's going to be hell for their cruisers to get onto the bridge, though, what with the pile-up our accident has caused. I have a little time.

"So, what? You're just gonna gank me and walk away? You don't think anyone will stop you?" the guy says. With blood covering his fake driver's uniform, he looks like something out of a horror film. His eyes are piercing, green, made that much starker by the shock of crimson splashed across his face. I feel like I should know who he is somehow. Like I've met him before. The mystery of his identity is hovering at the very edges of my mind. It'll come to me.

Now isn't the time to be racking my brain over some maybe meeting that took place god knows when, though. Now's the time to be kicking his ass and leaving as quickly as possible. I have to find that girl before she gets herself into even more trouble. McLaughlin won't see it as trouble she got herself into. It'll be trouble *I* got her into, and then subsequently failed to prevent from worsening. That's how Paddy works. You take ownership for something, you'd better fucking make sure you can take care of it, otherwise he's coming after you. And he's not the kind of person to chalk something up to shitty luck or an accident, either. He'll say that I should have *known*, like *knowing* is a supernatural gift that I must somehow possess.

"Come on," the guy says. "We need to get out of here before the cops show up. And, sweetheart, if you want to live, you won't make a fuss about it, okay?"

I want to throat punch this bastard. He comes at me, hands out in front of him like he's trying to calm a startled deer or something, and I snap. I am not a startled deer. I am the predator that springs the deer and rips its fucking throat out. This poor asshole can't know that, though. He can't know about the fourteen years of Krav Maga training I've had. He can't know about the army training I received in my late teens and early twenties. He can't know about the countless hours and hours I've spent at the range, shooting and throwing knives until missing is something I just don't do anymore.

He finds out pretty quickly, though.

He's reaching for my gun, like he thinks he's just going to be able to pluck it straight out of my hands. I wait until he's within arm's distance, and then I spin the gun around in my hand, gripping it by the muzzle, and I coldcock him with it right in the face. Blood explodes from his nose, his head kicking back.

The sirens sound closer.

When the guy looks up at me, hands cupped over his nose, his eyes are wide with disbelief. "You're gonna regret that, sweetheart."

"I don't know. I'm feeling pretty good about it." I shouldn't be baiting him, but he's an arrogant prick and I'm pretty sure he's dead set on killing me once he has me safely out of the public's eye. Stalking forward, he reaches into his jacket and pulls out a gun. It's a Berretta, an old one with a scuffed muzzle—clearly he's used a silencer on it once or twice before. No silencer now, though. He doesn't seem to notice that we're surrounded by people anymore. People with horrified expressions on their faces and cell phones in their hands, recording every single step we make. I watch his body, watch the way he moves. I'm trained to do that before I make assumptions about anyone. I come to the conclusion very quickly from the way he holds his gun, the way he holds himself—sure, confident, his weight over the back of his feet— that he's trained too. The way he steps one foot over the other is a typical army training move that could mean he served or he's just had the benefit of professional coaching. Either way, I don't plan on underestimating him.

When he lunges for me, I'm ready. I deflect the hand he was going to grab me with, slapping it downward, and then I grab onto his wrist, pulling him off balance. He seesaws forward but then rips his wrist out of my hand. I don't expect him to turn his slight fumble to his own advantage, but he does. Dropping to the floor, he rolls and kicks out, landing a solid strike to my leg. I have less than a second to brace myself before I'm hitting the concrete.

Then he's on top of me. "Oh, this is fun, sweetheart. But I don't really have time to be playing games with you right now."

He's reaching for my arms, about to pin me to the ground, but I jab, landing a solid hit with my extended fingertips right in the base of his throat, in his windpipe. He chokes, his body falling sideways, and then I'm on top of *him*. Through watering eyes and a clearly sore throat, the guy grins up at me, shaking his head. "Well, if you wanna fuck me, I guess I could *make* some time." Thrusting upward, he tries to unseat me, but I know this is what's coming and I'm ready again. I compensate, leaning forward, pressing my gun into the guy's neck.

"Who are you?"

His body goes still, his hands lifting so they're palm up in front of him. "You know who I am, sweetheart. I'm the enemy."

"My boss has quite a few enemy camps. Which one do you belong to?"

"The biggest one," the guy says, smiling. "The Italian one."

"So you work for Barbieri?"

"I *am* a Barbieri." Lightning fast, he snaps his hand out and clamps it around my throat. The move catches me off guard, has me panicking for the first time. My gun is gone, then, knocked to the ground, skittering away across the blacktop. The guy's hand tightens around the column of my neck, threatening to squeeze even harder. "What's wrong?" he asks. "Feeling a little lightheaded?"

I break his hold over me, smashing my fist into his solar plexus, winding him for the second time. He's good, though. We're both on our feet in a heartbeat. Again, he's already swinging his arm toward me, his fist clenched. I duck, but he leans back and kicks out, his shin striking me in the stomach, hard. He's breathing hard now. So am I. I lash out—a backhander that hits him on the temple, sending him reeling. My knee comes up automatically. Not to kick him in the balls, but to push him back as I bring my elbow down on his shoulder as hard as I can. I follow up with a back kick, strong enough to force him to retreat a few paces.

He counters, coming at me with ... with what looks like a length of black material. His tie? It was around his neck a minute ago and now it's in his hands, one end wrapped around his fist. He surges forward, on the attack, his clenched fist rounding on me, landing on my jaw. The force of the blow sends me to the ground. Hurts like a fucking bitch. I could jump up, but I don't. I wait for him, until he's standing right in front of me, breathing hard, before I thrust both feet up, kicking him in the stomach. He comes down on top of me, hands scrambling to get hold of my arms, but I don't stop moving. He can't catch hold of me if I keep my body fluid. I wrap an arm around his neck from behind, determination sweeping through me. I have to end this. I have to—

He shifts quickly, lifting his arms, flicking something over my head. He loops his hands one more time and I realize what he's done. He's looped the goddamn tie around my neck. I move fast, working to get a handful of the material before he can tighten it, but it's too late. He pulls, the narrow strip of silk constricting my airways, making it impossible to draw oxygen into my lungs.

I dig my knuckles into his groin—a seriously painful pressure point if you're a dude—but he doesn't let me go. He grunts, grinding his teeth, staring down at me as he keeps on pulling.

My head's beginning to swim. I try jabbing my fists into his side, but still he doesn't let go.

"Go to sleep, sweetheart. Thaaaat's right. Ha! *Holy fuck!* Crazy bitch." I can see the amusement in his eyes as my vision begins to fade. He knows he's won, and yet he seems surprised. I can barely believe it, myself. The last sound I hear before I fall unconscious is the staccato *blat blat blat* of gunfire ringing out across the George Washington Bridge. That, and the terrified screaming of the people standing around us.

THEO

I TAKE HER BACK TO THE RESTAURANT, EVEN THOUGH it's the worst fucking idea I've ever had. My knuckles are bleeding everywhere. They're stinging like a motherfucker as I lead the girl through the back into Cucina Diavolo. It'd be suicide taking her in through the front door. My father would take one look at the girl I'm dragging behind me and realize that his sons had fucked up again. The girl would get a bullet between the eyes and then so would I. If I was lucky. If was unlucky, I'd be getting my throat cut and enjoying a ride out to the pig farm my father keeps in Ulster County to fatten up his pork.

That sounds fucked up, and it is. Pigs are an excellent way of clearing up a mess, though. They'll eat anything. Accountants. Pimps. Prostitutes. Your progeny, if they crash a car on the George Washington Bridge and allow the teenaged daughter of your sworn enemy to escape.

Fuck.

The kitchen's busy. Luca, the head chef of the Barbieri family restaurant, doesn't look up as I drag my noncompliant friend through his workspace. His sous chef and the prep guys know the drill, too. I don't need to worry about any of them. They know better than to acknowledge anything dangerous. Anything that could end up in them witnessing something that could get them killed.

"Hey. Hey! One of you assholes better call the fucking cops. Hey, you. You with the knife. Look at me, damn it! *Hey!*" The boys don't listen as I pull the bodyguard through the exit and up the stairs that lead to the office and a number of storage rooms. I'll be able to hide my mistake for a couple of hours until I can figure out what to do next. I need to call my brother. Did he manage to find that stuck-up Irish bitch? Fuck knows. He better have, is all I can say.

Shoving the bodyguard into the room at the far end of the building, she swears under her breath, staggering as I let her go. I follow her inside and slam the door behind me. No one ever comes in here. It's the secondary dry store—full of flour and spices and shit Luca would only need if the first dry store ran low. The girl glares at me, rubbing at her neck.

"The hell you gonna do with me now?" she asks. "Kill me?"

"Sure," I tell her. She rolls her eyes, which is kind of sexy. She's lethal with those fists of hers, but her expressions are designed to kill, too.

"You're not going to kill me. You need me to tell you where Kaitlin would have gone."

She's right. I do need that from her. Sooner rather than later would be a bonus. "Why'd you bother asking, then?"

"To see if you were gonna flinch away from it. And since you didn't, I'm guessing you've got no problem with hurting women?"

"You aren't a damsel in distress, sweetheart. You nearly killed me."

"You wanna go another round? I feel like I was a little off my game before. What with having just been in a car crash and all."

"I think I'll pass. How about you sit down," I point to the drum of olive oil propped on one end against the wall, "and you and I can have that chat?"

"I don't know where she's gone. You should save your breath. And Paddy won't stump up ransom for me, if that's what you're thinking. He's like the American government. He doesn't negotiate with terrorists. Not for me. Not for his own daughter. Not for anyone."

"We don't want money."

"Then you must simply want to die. He's going to kill you all for this. You and your brother—I'm assuming he's your brother?—could leave the state right now, this second, and it wouldn't make a difference. He'll find you and he'll skin you alive."

"Sal and I aren't going anywhere."

"Then enjoy what's left of your life, moron."

"Gladly." I pull out my cell and hit the speed dial for Sal, waiting with bated breath for him to pick up. He doesn't, though. I let it ring and ring and ring, but I get no answer.

47

What the hell is he doing? We agreed a long time ago that we'd maintain contact in situations like this. How bad is it that we have an action plan in case of kidnappings gone wrong? Like this happens every goddamn weekend. "Where the fuck are you, man?" I growl under my breath.

"Boyfriend not picking up?" Tall and Beautiful asks.

"Shut up and sit your ass down," I snap. I haven't turned my back on her. She's dangerous and she knows how to fight. I don't intend on giving her the opportunity to hand my ass to me, escape the storeroom and vault out of a window or some shit. I've known her for all of five seconds but I feel like it's something she would do. I give up on the phone and slide it back into my pocket, giving her my full attention. "What's your name?"

"Why the hell should I tell you that?"

"Because I can find out easily enough, and you know not telling me would be a massive waste of time. The quicker we get through this, the quicker you can go."

She shakes her head, looking away. "You must think I'm mentally challenged."

"Are you? Most people who find themselves in this situation are less mouthy."

"Oh, honey. I've been in this situation more times than I can count. I'm not gonna dissolve into tears and start begging for my life."

"That's a pity. I do love when a woman begs me for things. And please ... feel free to call me honey again. I like how that sounds, too."

She probably meant to barb me with the name, to condescend me, but I wasn't lying. Her using that name on me sounded really fucking good. Like, way too good. I need to keep my focus here, but it's not easy with her covered in blood and sweat and her clothes clinging to her, looking sexy as all get out. If Sal were here, he'd have probably already cut off three of her fingers but we'd know her social security number, bra size, the name of her childhood family dog, the works. I could hazard a guess at her bra size—34C?—but other than that ...

"My name is Gracie O'Connor," she says, her voice turning cold. "Patrick McLaughlin has been taking care of me since I was a kid. You could say he considers me his blood. So the sooner you figure out what you're going to do with me and do it, the better. And by the way," she says, lifting her eyebrows. "You look at my chest one more time and we're gonna be having words."

I'm about to give her a few when I'm cut short by a knock at the door. So much for no one ever coming back here. Fuck. I press my shoulder against the wood, praying it's not Billie or Joseppi, or any of my father's other half-witted lackeys. Gracie O'Connor is giving me an unimpressed look when I shoot her a warning glance. "Do not make a fucking sound," I tell her.

"I'm trapped in enemy territory with Roberto Barbieri's men at every turn. I'm not a complete idiot," she hisses back.

"Theo? Theo, baby, I know you're in there. Come on, open the door."

Fuck. Shandi. Yeah, that's right, *Shandi*, like the drink but with an I instead of a Y. Total stripper name, which is exactly what Shandi was before my father decided to give her a job as a waitress in the restaurant. She wanted to clean up and Pops wanted a hot piece of ass working the floor to distract the diners from the comings and goings of New York City's underworld elite. I've fucked her a few times here in this very room, which is what she must be looking for now—a quick roll to make the day a little more interesting.

She won't go away. I know she won't. Gracie's eyebrows are arched, showing her disapproval. Shandi, on the other side of the door, somehow says the worst thing she possibly could say. She has a talent for that. "Come on, Theo, open the door. I wanna suck that beautiful dick, baby. My pussy's wet and you haven't licked her in a while."

I hate when women refer to their pussies as *her*. Gracie bites back laughter, rolling her eyes. "*Please*, lover boy. Don't stand on ceremony on my account. By all means, *go right ahead*."

CHAPTER FOUR
SAL

I CAN FEEL IT IN THE WAY MY HANDS ARE FIDGETING, the nervous dread locked in my gut like cement.

I'm about to lose my shit over this broad.

"Come on, smartass," I say, flicking my eyes over her. She's short, small tits, but they're perky underneath that ill-fitting sack she's wearing. Not so small that you couldn't stick your dick between them and go to town. "Where is she?"

Not that I'm thinking about that right now. Nope. This chick might be the hottest thing I've seen in a long time, dark hair and hazel-green eyes set just right in her pretty, heart-shaped face. But—and there's always a but—she looks like she's got a screw loose somewhere in there, and, oh yeah, she just lost my fucking mark. Kaitlin is probably halfway back to Hell's Kitchen by now, ready to tell Papa Paddy what we just did.

We're dead, the both of us. Me and Theo. Motherfucker! We should've just gone with my plan—chloroform the bitches the second they stepped off that plane. But Theo, man, he's always gotta do things his way.

And now we're completely fucking fucked.

I grind my teeth together, so hard I think they're going to crack under the pressure. Wouldn't be the first time. My dentist says I carry all my stress in my jaw.

I lean in real close to her, crowding her. How we're still the only two people in this room, I have no frigging clue. I can only guess the manager woman I saw out the front doesn't want cops poking around the back of her diner and has pointed them off in some other direction. Still, doesn't explain why nobody else has come looking. When I ran back here, chasing the Irish bitch that slipped through my fingers, the whole diner seemed to turn and gawk as I flew through. I mean, I'm not exactly easy to miss. All six-four of me, and especially since I'm still wearing the goddamn driver's suit and hat. How it didn't fall off in the crash is anyone's guess.

"Where. Is. She?" I demand, enunciating every word, every syllable, because I'm *this close* to smashing her face in, woman or not. Every second she screws around and bats her eyelashes at me is a second Kaitlin McLaughlin is running her blonde ass further away, and taking with her any hopes of my brother and I making it out of this fix unscathed.

Briefly, I wonder which one of them will kill us. Roberto or Paddy. Our father or hers. Maybe they'll take one each. A bullet in the head, a nice swim in the Hudson with our feet encased in quick-set concrete. We'll sink like stones to the bottom of the dirty river, frozen like caricatures of our former selves, while the fish eat out our eyes and our flesh sloughs off with rot and the shifting tides. Until finally, we're two skeletons standing at the bottom of the deep brown riverbed, our bones gently swaying in the wake of the ferries that cut across the harbor every few minutes, our skulls grinning maniacally without flesh to hide our teeth.

"Suck my dick," she says, her eyes alight with something—with satisfaction? What a strange creature she is. Most other women in this situation would scream and cry and beg, but not this one. She's got this aura about her that makes me wonder what happened to her, how exactly life crushed her. Yeah. That's it. She looks crushed. She looks ... empty.

I pull my head back a little, certain what I heard isn't what she said.

"Pardon me?" I ask, fighting the urge to laugh. She didn't say that. Words like that don't come out of mouths as perfect as hers. God, where do I know her from?

She smiles, but the gesture is completely devoid of warmth. For the first time since I ran into this bathroom stall, I'm beginning to wonder what exactly the fuck I'm dealing with here. There is something seriously off about this chick.

"I said, suck my big, fat, dirty dick," she spits, her green eyes flashing with emotion. "And while you're at it, kiss my ass, too. She's long gone, sunshine."

My jaw just about falls on the fucking floor. "Who are you?" I ask, more to myself than to her. I must have screwed this chick and I just don't remember. I've taken plenty of chicks back to my place on Bleecker Street and made them do the walk of shame the next morning—I don't snuggle after I fuck. That's *got* to be it.

"Did you just call me *sunshine?*" I add. I can feel this situation careening out of control, much like the car when it flipped over on the fucking bridge five minutes ago.

"Are you deaf or something?" she bites back, her smug smile vanishing.

I lean closer again, catch a whiff of the coffee on her breath. And something else. Vodka. *Ahhh.* "You're drunk at eight-thirty in the morning?" I ask incredulously.

She huffs, a laugh that contains no real emotion, just a defensive reflex. "Are you judging me, gangster boy?"

I raise my eyebrows. As much as I want to keep bantering with this broad, I've got an Irish bitch to bag before I end up in a body bag. "Time's up," I growl, pressing my gun into her sternum, right along the line of buttons between her breasts.

She clamps her mouth shut, her stance insolent, her eyes narrowed.

And I snap.

"Time to go for a little drive then, sweetheart," I grimace, shifting the gun so it's digging into the side of her ribs.

"You're sweating," she says casually.

Who the fuck is this woman? My dick wants to find out. The rest of me? I'm not so sure. She's so unhinged, she's almost ... scaring me. "It's hot," I reply. Why am I even answering her? Fuck that. "Walk," I demand, pulling her alongside me. I loop my arm around her shoulder so we're walking side by side, shifting the gun so it's now underneath my suit jacket, still pointed firmly into her side. "What's your name?" I hiss.

She just glares up at me. "Petunia," she drawls. "What's yours?"

I huff. "Your name is not ..." I struggle to even repeat the word, it's so ridiculous. "*Petunia.*"

She just shrugs. This chick is mad. She's certifiable. I should just shoot her in her pretty face and make a run for it. Still, she'll be handy as a hostage if it comes to that. The mood in the diner wasn't exactly joyous when I ran through, bleeding and chasing Kaitlin. Why has nobody come to check on her? Are there cops out there, right now? I gotta chance it. I have to get out of here. My neck's starting to itch, almost as much as my trigger finger.

I've got that feeling in my gut. The one that tells me I'll be emptying my clip before the day's finished. Hopefully into somebody else, and not into my own skull.

We make our way out of the bathroom and past the kitchen, where the fat Russian guy is throwing giant slabs of butter onto a hotplate. He's oblivious, and I have to wonder if I was just imagining the looks I got when I ran through the diner after Kaitlin.

We're almost at the door when a squat Italian woman steps in front of us, her face thunderous.

"Scarlett! You've got tables to clear," she growls, snapping her fingers in front of this chick's face.

Scarlett. Oh, Christ. I can just imagine the way her cheeks turn *scarlet* red when she's coming, my face between her legs. Oh, fuck. Focus, Barbieri!

"I'm being abducted," Scarlett says to her boss, glancing

up at me. "Can't you ask Helen to clear my section? She's already taken my tips."

I almost choke. *I'm being abducted?*

"Honey, didn't you tell your boss I was coming to visit today? It *is* our anniversary, you know."

The squat woman smiles up at me, and I shoot back a placating grin, with as much charm as I can muster right now. "Scarlett, you didn't tell me you were dating *Salvatore!*"

And the smile falls right the fuck off my face. I can't go anywhere in this damn city without being recognized.

Satisfaction spreads across Scarlett's face as she looks up at me with a grin. "Salvatore," she says, her voice saccharine sweet.

"How long have you two been together?" the woman asks, her eyes flicking between Scarlett and me, almost in disbelief.

"Coming up to five minutes now," Scarlett replies casually.

The woman shakes her head. "When I saw you come in, I thought for sure you were one of those *stronzo* cab drivers using our toilet to take a dump."

"Oh, he did," Scarlett says, deadpan even with a gun pressed against her right tit. *Fascinating.* "He's got violent diarrhea. He just destroyed one of the bathroom stalls."

Well, I don't know what to say to *that.* "We need to go." I pull Scarlett firmly past her boss. "Scar forgot her crazy pills this morning. She might be back in tomorrow."

"What? You're working a double today!" the woman screeches, but I ignore her, kicking the heavy glass door open and escaping into the stream of people clogging the sidewalk.

We need a cab. We need a cab right fucking now.

"Where are we going?" Scarlett asks.

I pull her over to the street and hail down a cab. "For a drive."

"Where?"

"Just get into the damn cab," I say, releasing my stronghold on her long enough to shove her into the backseat of the waiting cab before sliding in behind her.

The driver starts heading up the busy street. "Where to?" he calls through the small slot in the Plexiglas.

"Just keep heading up here," I say. "Head to Bleecker." If the bitch won't tell me where she's hiding Kaitlin, she's coming home with me until I can break her resolve. I groan inwardly. I really, really can't be bothered torturing someone today. It's Friday, I'm hung over as fuck, and there's a very real possibility that there's still a naked woman in my bed at home.

"You're sweating on me," she remarks, wriggling away on the plastic-covered bench seat. I tut, pulling her even closer. Has she got a problem with sweat? I mean, it's not pouring off me—I'm just perspiring a little underneath all these clothes. "It's summer, baby. We all sweat. I bet you're sweating right now under that sack you call a dress. And if you're not," I give her a sidelong grin, "we can certainly fix that."

God, I'd like to get her hot and sweaty.

"Don't call me baby," she says, clearly unimpressed. "I'm *not* your baby."

"Sorry, *Petunia*." I roll my eyes, snickering. I look up ahead, my phone vibrating in my suit pocket, the *Game of Thrones* theme song sounding obnoxiously through the cab. It's been ringing on and off since we first got into the cab.

"Aren't you going to get that?" Scarlett asks.

I smile condescendingly. "The only way I'm taking my attention off you is if you're face down in my lap with your mouth open, and somehow I think we should wait until our fifteen-minute anniversary for that."

Bitch doesn't even bristle. "You know, you could just silence it before I shoot myself in the face over here."

I shrug incredulously. "It's the *Game of Thrones* theme music. Who doesn't like *Game of Thrones?*"

She stares at me angrily, and it suddenly slams home.

"I didn't fuck you at all," I exclaim. She's not one of those broads I wined, dined and sixty-nined before kicking out of my house. She's Scarlett *fucking* Winchester.

"You wish," she mutters under her breath. I'd normally snap off a witty retort, but she's Scarlett fucking Winchester.

"You're that chick out of that show!" I say excitedly. I don't add the fact that I've jerked off to the image of her character more times than I can count. This is just fucking bizarre.

She takes a deep breath and stares straight ahead. I frown. "You look ... different than you used to. Hey, what the hell happened to you? You just disappeared. Did you stop sucking the director's dick or something?"

She presses her fingers to her closed eyes. "Are you going to kill me?" she hisses, low enough that the cab driver can't hear. "Because if that's your plan, can we skip the small talk and get to the killing part?"

Shit. She's not joking. Her words leave me reeling for a moment. Not only have Theo and I just lost the bitch we were supposed to kidnap, crashed our limo, and probably earned ourselves each a bullet in the skull, but I've also managed to take a hostage who's suicidal.

I chew on the inside of my cheek, tasting blood. This is not good. It's so far from good, we're not even in the same realm as good. We're not good, we're not OK, we're not anything except completely screwed. We're dead men.

I'm too young and pretty to die.

"Cat got your tongue?" Scarlett asks, her hands back in her lap and her eyes on me. My cock stirs in my suit pants. *Oh, your pussy can have my tongue, Scarlett fucking Winchester. Meow.*

Down, boy. My cock's timing is terrible. I don't dignify her retort with a response.

Peering out of the window, I see a familiar sight. "Pull into this driveway," I urge the cab driver, tapping the glass that separates us. I turn to Scarlett, whose attention has pricked up as she studies our path. Looking for an escape? Jesus. I can't handle her and the cabbie at the same time. The numbers aren't matching up.

"You gonna behave?" I ask, jabbing her with the gun again.

"Bite me," she replies. I'd definitely bite her nipples if I could just get my mouth near them. But I need to stop thinking about nipples right now.

Great. Well. *This* is happening.

"Happy ten-minute anniversary," I hiss, shoving the gun down the front of my pants and lunging for her as covertly as I can. I don't need the cab driver seeing me attacking this girl and raising the alarm. Scarlett's body tenses immediately, and her hands fly out, trying to push me away, but I've got more upper body weight than she's got in her entire body. I over-power her easily, using my elbows to pin her arms to her sides, my palms at her neck as I press down on her carotid artery. Her eyes go wide, and she opens her mouth to scream.

"Sorry, sweetheart," I murmur. "I'll make you scream if you want, but not right now." I lean in, covering her mouth with mine, kissing her to drown out the noise of her cry for help. She tastes like I thought she would—coffee and vodka. Irish coffee, isn't that what they call it? My stomach roils at the Irish part. Fucking Kaitlin. I'm going to find *that* bitch, even if I have to tie *this* bitch to a chair and torture the address out of her.

I continue applying pressure to the sweet spot in her neck, cutting off the blood flow from her heart to her brain just for a few seconds. It doesn't take long before she's a dead weight in my arms, her eyes lolling back in her head before fluttering shut.

I release her mouth, letting her slide down the back of the seat so she's lying across it, her thighs slightly parted and her legs off to the side as her feet rest awkwardly on the floor.

"She okay?" the cab driver asks, tapping on the Plexiglas. I hold my hands up in mock surprise. "I don't know, man. She's diabetic. I think she's having a fit or something."

The cab driver looks vaguely annoyed, but to his credit he unbuckles his belt, steps out of his door and circles around to mine. He opens the door and peers in.

"Need me to call an ambulance?" he asks.

I raise my gun to his forehead. "No, thanks," I reply, pressing the gun against his head. "Keys, please."

He points to the ignition. "They're still in there, asshole."

I smile broadly as I unfold myself, stepping out of the open door and into the alleyway I've directed him down. "Excellent. Open the trunk, please."

The annoyed look on his face morphs into actual fear. "Hey, man, just take the car, okay? It's insured. I won't say nothing to nobody. Hell, I didn't even see you."

If only that were the truth. "It's okay," I say. "I won't kill you. But I really need you to open that trunk."

He looks past me to Scarlett, lying unconscious on the backseat. "You gonna put her in there?" he asks, his tone almost hopeful.

"Sure," I lie. He looks relieved. I fight the urge to smack him out. I'll be able to do that in just a moment.

"Hurry," I urge, shaking the gun at him. With great reluctance, he reaches in through his open driver's door and presses a button.

"It's open," he says, and if Scarlett thought I was sweating, she obviously hasn't seen the river pouring off this guy's shiny bald forehead. He's freaking the fuck out.

"Go round and open it up," I say, my eyes never leaving his.

"I got heart problems," he says. "I can't be in confined spaces!"

I raise my eyebrows at him. "Get in," I demand, pushing him toward the trunk and smacking the back of his head with the side of the Glock. He yelps, covering his head with his hands. "Okay, okay."

He clambers in awkwardly, until finally he's on his side in the trunk.

"If you have a heart attack in there, I'll kill you," I say, slamming the trunk forcefully.

I make my way to the driver's door, pausing to shut the door I just used to exit the backseat. Scarlett's still sleeping like a baby, her chest rising and falling in slow, even breaths. I didn't kill her with my little artery trick. Thank Christ. She's of no use to me dead.

I get in the driver's seat and push the chair back, catching a glance of myself in the rearview mirror. I'm still wearing my driver's cap.

How fitting.

I tip my cap to myself in the mirror, take the emergency brake off, and ease the car back into the busy morning traffic; my soundtrack the oscillating ringtone of my brother's desperation.

CHAPTER FIVE
SCARLETT

WHEN I COME TO, MY NECK FEELS TENDER, BRUISED almost. I look around, wondering where the fuck I've ended up today. It wouldn't be the first time I've passed out and forgotten where I am.

A steady diet of booze and pills will do that to a person.

I scrub my hand across my face, the gesture meant to make my vision clearer somehow, but it doesn't work. My eyes feel crusty, my mouth is dry as fuck, and I can hear someone singing along to a song about city boys born and raised in south Detroit.

And then I remember.

I sit bolt upright, taking a huge gasp of air in as I do so. Salvatore is driving, still wearing that ridiculous-looking cap as he sings off-key. I take in the buildings outside as they pass by, quickly recognizing the Meatpacking District. My guess is proven correct when I catch sight of a sign for Bleecker Street. We haven't gone far, which makes me hopeful that I can still somehow get out of this pinch. But first ... Something's missing. Something isn't right.

"Where's the driver?" I ask dumbly, scanning the backseat. No answer. I realize he can't hear me through the Plexiglas that separates us, especially with the music turned up so loud. I pound my fist into the clear divider to get his attention. "Hey, motherfucker!" I yell.

He turns and flashes me a grin. "Good morning, Scarlett *Winchester.*" His voice is muffled somewhat by the divider, but I can still hear well enough as he drawls my name. He lets the syllables roll slowly off his tongue like he's my best friend, or my lover, and that's annoying. Especially since it's not even my real name. Scarlett Smith was far too boring for Hollywood casting agents, and my daddy liked to collect rare guns. I was almost Scarlett Colt, until I did some googling and found out Scarlett Colt was a porn star whose signature move was shooting bullets out of her ... well, you know.

Scarlett Winchester seemed the better choice.

"Where are you taking me?" I yell. "Where's the driver?"

I try my door handle. Locked. And there's no mechanism to unlock it, since we're in the back of a city cab. Fuck.

He shrugs, almost amused as he holds up one finger. "Wait, this is the best part," he says, turning the music up so loud, it's gonna make my ears bleed. He starts singing/ screaming about strangers and boulevards and street lights. He's a terrible singer, but he's got me so distracted, I don't even notice him pulling the cab into a basement parking lot, my eyes wide with horror as I watch a heavy garage door closing us in.

Fuck. How much of an idiot am I? I've just let this guy take me from work. I can't afford the day off. I need those fucking tips to pay for my little pill habit.

Okay, my large, ugly pill habit. Whatever.

I swallow thickly as Sal shuts the car off, his expression serious as he gets out of the car and slams his door. I'm crawling back on my hands as he opens my door, his smile so congenial it's almost reassuring.

"Get out," he says, offering a hand to me. I kick his hand with my foot, but he's too fast, catching my ankle as something dark flashes in his eyes. His other hand comes into the car, and it's pointing a gun at me.

"Please," he adds, his smile completely gone.

"I can't move," I sulk. "You've got my foot."

He smiles dangerously, loosening his grip on my ankle. He slides his hand from my skin ever so slowly, offering it again. "Come on," he says. "I've got plenty of alcohol for you, if that's what it'll take to get you to talk."

My mouth practically waters at the suggestion.

He laughs. "Come on, Scarlett Petunia. I've got a busy fucking day ahead."

I frown, pushing his hand away as I clamber out of the car.

It's a short elevator ride to his apartment, my legs feeling like lead as I'm marched in front of the gun-wielding Salvatore. It's just starting to hit me, how fucked up this whole situation is. I'm in deep shit, and it's only getting worse. As the elevator opens and Sal presses me with the tip of his gun to get out, I freeze.

He's gonna kill me. He's gonna get the address out of me, and then he's gonna shoot me in the head.

Worryingly, the thought doesn't scare me as much as it should. It does scare me, but I feel oddly detached from my body, almost like I'm in shock.

Sal responds by taking a handful of my hair and pulling me along beside him. I struggle at first, my hands going up into my hair and trying to pry his fingers free, but it's a losing battle. I have two choices: let him lead me into this place, or let him tear my entire scalp off my skull.

I choose the first one.

The elevator closes behind us, and the loud noise of people fucking fills my ears. I listen for a moment, feeling oddly invasive, almost as if I'm eavesdropping on people while they go at it like rabbits. The chick isn't just moaning—she's screaming.

Wait, no, that's not right. There are two female voices. One is moaning along with the guy, but the second female voice is screaming a name.

"Sal. Sal! I know you're here! Get your fucking ass up here and untie me!"

I move my gaze slowly to Sal, feeling as if I'm in some screwed-up dream. The color drains from his face as he hears his name being called.

"Oh, motherfucker," he swears, looking upstairs.

"What is that?" I whisper. I feel like whispering is the most appropriate thing to do in this situation.

"Nothing," Sal says, waving his hand dismissively.

"Salvatore Barbieri!" the female voice yells.

"I'm coming!" Salvatore screams back up the stairs.

I can't help it. I start to laugh, and maybe I'm still just super nervous and fearing for my life, but the moaning, coupled with Sal screaming that he's coming, just about has *me* coming undone at the sides with giggles.

"What's so funny?" Sal asks me, clearly having missed the joke.

"Sal!" the woman's voice screams again.

"I said *I'm coming!*" Sal barks, catching on as he looks at me again. I see the edge of his mouth twitch as he hears what he's saying.

"Are we in a brothel?" I whisper. "Where's the cab driver?"

Sal shakes his head in disbelief. "Do you know him or something?" he asks. I shake my head back, dragging my feet as he takes hold of my arm and starts hauling me up a sweeping mahogany staircase, toward the source of the screaming and moaning.

"Then why do you care?" he asks. "He's fine. He's in the trunk of the cab. Once this is all over, I'll send him home with his car and he'll. Be. Fine."

"Huh," I huff, secretly glad I'm not in the trunk of a cab.

The moaning reaches fever pitch as the voice screams out, "Sal! Get this thing out of my pussy!"

I almost choke when I hear what she's said. I look at Sal, whose cheeks are so, so red they might as well have been lit on fire. He clears his throat, looking nervous as we reach the top of the stairs.

I have a feeling that things are about to get even more

fucked up.

And, sure enough, I'm right.

We enter a large bedroom at the top of the stairs, and I finally see the source of all the noise. It's a nice bedroom as far as rooms go, but it smells ... it smells like piss. There's a large bed against one wall, an impressive four-poster affair. Oh, yeah, and there's a chick lying—tied—to each bedpost, stark naked, a giant black vibrator stuck up her ... well, you know.

"You motherfucking motherfucker!" the chick screams at Sal, her eyes wild, her face smeared with old makeup. I look at Sal, who appears hopelessly lost.

"Katya," he says awkwardly. "You're still here?"

The chick looks like she's about to pop a blood vessel. The moaning and breathing is so loud, and it's not coming from her. I scan the room, my eyes landing upon a large flat-screen television hanging on the wall, with porn playing loudly.

"You fucking tied me up!" she screams, rattling the ropes on her wrists to make her point.

"I did sailors' knots," he says. "I thought you knew how to undo them."

She just glares at him.

I'm still transfixed by the bizarre situation when Sal takes my elbow and leads me past the bed, shoving me down into a chair. I don't struggle until I see a length of rope appear in his hands—the same rope securing Miss Porn Star to the bed.

"Oh, no fucking way, buddy!" I protest, pulling my hands away. "I'm not letting you do that to me!"

Sal responds by covering my mouth and nose with his large palm, pinching my nose shut and sealing off my mouth so I can't breathe.

Really, again? That's what I want to say, but obviously I can't since I'm silenced by his hand, not to mention on the verge of passing the fuck out again. I kick his shins with my cheap work shoes, pummel his face with my fists, but it's no use. He had the jump on me, and I'm clearly not at my best, the first pains of needing one of those magic white pills starting to eat into my bones. My eyes start to flutter closed and all the fight goes out of me as I slump forward against Sal's hard chest. I'm still hovering on the edge of consciousness, but it's like I'm drunk, my limbs heavy and clumsy as I attempt to push him away. It's useless, though. By the time he takes his hand away and I can suck in a great lungful of air, I'm tied to this stupid chair.

"Sal!" the chick on the bed screams. I catch another acidic whiff as I'm desperately filling my lungs, and, yeah, I'm pretty fucking sure she pissed the bed.

CHAPTER SIX
THEO

BLONDE. CURVES. LEGS UP TO HER GODDAMN ARM-
pits. Tits blatantly on show for me. The woman standing on
the other side of the door is sex personified. Normally I get
hard just looking at her, but not now. Not when there's a
belligerent Gracie O'Connor standing behind me, just
waiting for an opportunity to kick my ass, and I can't fucking
find my tearaway brother.

Shandi pouts, shoving out her chest. "Luca said you came
up here," she informs me in that husky voice of hers. "You said
you'd come find me when you got back, baby. What are you
doing up here all alone?"

So Luca told her I was up here but he failed to mention I
wasn't alone. I could kiss the man. Shandi and I aren't
together but I don't think she'd mind it if we were. I would,
though. Bitch is crazy. "I just needed to make a phone call. It's

private up here, is all," I say.

Shandi runs her hand up my chest, making a sound at the back of her throat that comes close to a purr. "Don't I know it, baby. Come on. Let's have some fun, huh?" She tries to push me back into the room so she can come inside but I anchor on, bracing one hand against the doorframe. "Now's not really a good time, Shan. I have to find Sal." To my credit, this is true.

Shandi doesn't seem to care for my honesty, though. "You've bent me over and fucked me in there at least five times when *I've* had to go, Theo. I took a reaming from your dad last week when I was late, just so you could get your dick wet. It's time to return the favor, okay?" She poses the last bit as a question, but aside from her voice going up at the end, it's very clear she's not really asking. She wants to get fucked right here and right now, and she's determined to get her way.

She pushes harder against my chest, but I ain't budging. When she realizes this she moves quickly, ducking under my arm and slipping into the storeroom beyond. I reach for her, grabbing for her arm, but it's too late. She's already inside.

"Shan, don't—" I'm about to tell her not to make a scene, not to start screaming at me, asking who the random woman is sitting on the drum of olive oil, but I don't need to. Because Gracie is gone.

What. The. Actual. Fuck?

There are no windows in here. No trapdoors or secret exits. No way for Gracie to have physically made it out of the room. That means she must still be—

I see the white flash of her eyes in the darkness; she's

hiding between the wall and the five-tier shelving unit, cluttered with jars and pots of dried ingredients, clutching at her shoulder, like it's hurting her or something. I can barely make out the dark line of her body. Smart woman. She knows she's not getting out of here without getting shot, so no point trying to make a break for it. But she also knows that if she does manage to escape the storeroom, she'll then find herself in the household of her enemy, and they won't be as interested in keeping her alive as I am. I think I see her roll her eyes.

Shandi, god bless her blonde, unobservant heart, hasn't noticed the figure lurking in the corner. Her back is to Gracie so that she's facing me. And she's unbuttoning her waitress's shirt.

"Shan, I told you I don't have time. Later, after shift."

She pouts again, shaking her head. "But I want you now, baby. Why are you being so mean?" Her shirt's unbuttoned all the way now. Stronger men than me have crumpled to her feet at the sight of that cleavage. I know as soon as she unfastens that bra and loses it altogether I'm in serious shit. I can't let it happen. I pull the door to the storeroom closed and then take hold of her by the wrists. I can feel Gracie's eyes burning into the side of my head, daring me to even touch this woman while she's forced to watch.

The thought of that ... the thought of her having to watch me fuck this insanely attractive yet very annoying woman? I'm not gonna lie. It appeals to me in ways I can't even begin to describe. Gracie's been nothing but a pain since the moment she sat that perfect little ass of hers down in the back of the Lincoln. Fucking Shan in front of her when she can do absolutely nothing about it would definitely be one way to teach her to fucking behave herself. I can't justify wasting the time, though. Salvatore isn't exactly known for making good choices. He could be neck deep in shit right now and me fucking with either one of these girls isn't going to help matters.

"I told you. After shift, Shan." I apply a little pressure to her wrists—a warning. I should know better than to expect her to take heed of it. Instead, she smiles, licking her lips and then biting down on the bottom one. She should have worked in porn. Who the fuck knows? She probably has at some point. "Baby, you're making me angry," she says in the same childish whimper she uses on my father when she wants to finish a shift early. "You don't want to make me angry, do you? I run my mouth when I get angry. Say things I shouldn't. I let things slip."

My grip on her wrists tightens. "Don't fuck around. If you're trying to bribe me into sticking my dick into you, say it plainly. I don't like fucking games."

"Okay," she says, a serious look marshaling her features. I can still feel the lust boiling underneath the surface, but she seems cooler now. More focused. "If you don't screw me right now, I'll tell Roberto about Clara."

"Clara?" It feels like a stone weight is pulling at my insides, pulling me down, down, down. "What the fuck you mean, you'll tell him about *Clara?*" Clara is the thirty-eight-year-old woman my sixty-seven-year-old father has been fucking the past few months. He's obsessed with her, and Clara is obsessed with money. Their arrangement seems to work quite well, since Clara gives up her pussy at the very first sign of a dollar bill, and my father is rich as fuck. The woman is a viper, pure and simple. Both Sal and I steer well clear of her. Shan gives me a tease of a smile and I can practically hear the slow grind of the cogs turning in her head.

"Well, I'll tell him you've been fucking her, of course."

"I haven't even looked sideways at Clara."

"*I* know that, and *you* know that. But planting that seed in Roberto's head? That might be a bad thing, don't you think?" Shan laughs, like she's insanely pleased with herself for coming up with this foolproof plan to bend me to her will. If there's one thing she should have learned about me by now, though, it's that I don't bend to anybody's will. Not without a fight. I take a step toward her, glaring at her from under drawn brows. The laughter dies on her lips.

"What do you say, baby? You gonna give in and play with me now?" she asks, though she looks doubtful, as though she's suddenly realized what she's done.

I'm still glaring at her, fury in my eyes, as I walk her backward toward the oil drum. Spinning her around so I can sit down, I realize that she might end up seeing Gracie after all—she's to my right, still mostly hidden in the shadows—but I don't care anymore. I won't be blackmailed. Especially by Shandi. No fucking way. I'm gripping her wrists hard enough that my fingers have gone white now. She's starting to look a little concerned.

"Come here," I say, pulling her closer. "Bend yourself over my knee."

"What?"

"Bend yourself ... over my knee," I repeat slowly, waiting for her to oblige me. She does, slowly, eyes not leaving mine until the last second, and then her chest is pressing against my legs, her butt sticking up in the air, and I can feel her heart beat *thum, thum, thum*ming against my thighs. She's absolutely still as she braces herself, waiting to see if this is something she will like or something she will intensely dislike. I'm a sick bastard. The more she doesn't enjoy this, the more I'm going to.

"Theo?"

I grab the hem of her way-too-high black pencil skirt and yank it up over her ass. "I don't wanna hear another single word come out of your mouth," I say.

"But—" I grab hold of her panties next—surprised she's even wearing any—and I pull on them, hard. "Ahhh! Ow!" she cries out, like she's surprised that I'm being rough with her right after she's just threatened to tell my father something that would most likely get me killed.

"Not another word, Shan. Shut your fucking mouth." And she does. I think she finally, *finally* understands that her threat hasn't been received the way she was hoping. She goes still, as though she's weighing up her options: whether she should stay bent double over my legs with her naked ass in the air, or whether she should bolt. I look up and I catch Gracie staring at me ... at the hand I'm raising ... bringing down on Shan's bare backside. The tiny storeroom fills with the cracking sound of my palm meeting her flesh, and then her strangled, startled cry. Leaning down, I'm still staring Gracie in the eye as I whisper to Shan, "You should know better than to threaten me, sweetheart."

I spank her again, just as hard, still watching Gracie. The other woman just stands there with her back to the wall, watching, a blank look on her face. Her features are completely flat, but there's something there ... a light in her eyes that makes me want to smile like a maniac. She's not as disapproving as I thought she would be. In fact, I'm pretty sure, despite how badly she doesn't want me to know it, Gracie might actually be a little fascinated by what I'm doing right now. She's literally squirming.

Oh, really? Well, aren't you just one surprise after another, Miss O'Connor? I can barely fight the grim smile that spreads across my face as I raise my hand and bring it down on Shan's ass again. She cries out, her voice a mixture of outrage and frustrated pleasure. She digs her fingernails into my thigh, sharp enough to sting a little, and so I slap her again, this time a little lower. This time in between her legs, on the exposed flesh of her pussy. She's wet, of course. No surprises there. The girl doesn't even have the common sense not to be turned on while I'm reprimanding her. She yelps, her surprise catching in her throat and sticking there, cutting off as she holds her breath. I'm transfixed by Gracie—by the blush I can just about see building in her cheeks. By the way she's balled her hands into fists. By the cool yet very interested curiosity in those dark eyes of hers.

I can't resist it. I spank Shan again, eliciting the same response from her, but this time I leave my hand in place, fingers teasing over the slick, swollen flesh between her legs. Shan's anger quickly dissipates as I move my fingers, sliding them over her pussy, upward until I find the tight, firm bud of her clit. After that, she's back to purring again, annoyance forgotten as I work my middle finger in a tight circle over her pleasure center.

And Gracie watches.

Never in a million years did I expect this to happen. Today has been a hell of a day and it's not even mid-morning yet. And now this chick is actually watching me tease Shandi-with-a-fucking-I, like ... like she's wishing it was *her* over my knee? No. No way. Can't be.

"Oh my god. Fuck, Theo. I knew you wouldn't hold out on me." Shan squirms, reminding me of her presence, of what my hands are automatically doing to her. I smack her left butt cheek, making her squeak. I don't want to make her come. She doesn't fucking deserve it. But when I catch sight of Gracie's lips parting, her tongue slowly wetting them, I'm gripped by an overwhelming desire to know what she'll do if Shan *does* come. I'm beginning to think she'd enjoy it.

I have to find out. Pushing at the insides of her thighs, I make Shan spread her legs a little so I have better access to her ... and so Gracie can see what I'm doing. Slowly, so slowly, I slide my index and middle finger inside. She shivers, her body trembling. She makes a sound I'm more than used to—a stuttering sigh that means she's really enjoying herself now. But is Gracie?

Hard to tell. Her eyes are locked on my hand, on Shan's naked skin, but it looks like her chest is rising and falling a little faster. I see her hand twitch, a slight inward motion, and then she's uncurling her fist. She presses her open palm against the top of her thigh, wiping it, as though she's suffering from sweaty palms. She shifts it sideways, tips of her fingers digging into her pants, and I know it. I fucking *know* it. She wants to touch herself. She wants to slip her hand down the front of her pants, and she wants to run her fingers over her pussy the same way I'm running mine over Shan's. My dick was hard before, but all of a sudden it's made out of fucking granite. I can't think of anything I want to see more than that right now.

Gracie's eyes flicker up to mine, irritation clear as day in her expression, as though she knows she's been busted and she's mad about it. I smile a smile that feels about as wicked as they come. She looks away, closes her eyes, but I can tell that it takes effort.

"Do it," I say out loud.

Shan twists her head, trying to look over her shoulder. "Do what?" she pants. Without looking at her I grab hold of the back of her head and turn it away from me. I don't want to look at her and I sure as shit don't want her looking at me. I don't want her finally noticing Gracie, either. That would ruin the fun.

"*Do it*," I repeat, my voice low. "You know you want to." Gracie opens her eyes and looks at me, and I can see immediately that I'm right. She *does* want to.

"Okay. Okay, I'll come," Shan pants. "I'll come just for you, baby."

Better make it a good one, bitch. It's gonna be the last fucking time, I tell her in my head. I move my fingers quicker, plunging them inside her while reaching down with my thumb so I can rub her clit at the same time. That does the trick. Shan starts grinding her hips, rocking against my hand, her breathing becoming more and more labored as she draws closer to coming.

Gracie watches all of this without blinking. Her hand's right where she left it, fingers just shy of touching herself. I can't look away from her. I haven't touched my cock once and I think that can only be a good thing. If I were to take myself in my palm and stroke, I'd be fucked. And I pride myself on my staying power. I can hold off as long as I want to normally, but watching this woman on the brink of giving in and doing something seriously crazy is enough to destroy any hope I'd have of lasting more than five seconds.

Gracie looks at me again and I mouth it at her: *do it!* And then, in my head, *dear God, please fucking do it.*

Gracie's head tips back, her jaw angled upward, making her neck long and beautiful, and she locks a furious gaze on me. Her lips part even further and then she's mouthing something at me.

Fuck.

You.

I almost laugh. So she's not going to make herself come for me after all. That's a crying fucking shame, but I'm digging her attitude anyway. Just the shape of the word *fuck* on her mouth is enough to drive me crazy. I have to stop myself from throwing Shan off my lap and charging straight over there so I can lick and suck at the skin of her neck.

All thoughts of my father, of Kaitlin, of Salvatore go up in smoke as I pump my fingers into Shan. As she begins to tremble even harder, so does Gracie.

Shan's about to come. She's always been a screamer. She starts swearing, describing in haltering detail what she wants me to do to her as her pleasure washes over her. Gracie, on the other hand, bites her lip, pressing so hard with her teeth that her skin turns white. She sags against the wall, sweat beaded on her forehead, and I can tell she's feeling something right now. I'm not sure what, but she's definitely feeling *something*. The moment is over almost as quickly as it started when Shan sinks back on her heels, grinning up at me. Her eyeliner is smudged, running down her face. She looks like she just got royally fucked.

"Thank you, Theo," she says. "Started off a little weird there but I liked the end very much."

"Leave," I command.

She doesn't seem fazed now that she's gotten what she was after. She does give my dick a cursory squeeze as she gets unsteadily to her feet, though. "Damn, baby, you're rock hard. Are you sure you don't want me to blow you?"

I give her my shittiest, nastiest smile. "I'd rather you didn't, actually."

Shrugging, she pulls her skirt back down, not bothering to put her panties back on. "Whatever, baby." Kissing me roughly on the cheek, she then heads for the door. "By the way, your dad's looking for you."

I barely notice her leaving. My eyes are still fixed on the woman hiding herself behind the shelving. I do hear the door close, though. As soon as Shan's gone, I stand and face Gracie. I'm pretty sure my hard on would be visible from outer fucking space right now. She raises an eyebrow at me, lifting one shoulder.

"Oh, you wanna look at me like that, do you, sweetheart?" I growl. "You gonna tell me that didn't get you off even just a little bit?"

"You're fucking disgusting. Of course it didn't," she replies. But I can see it on her face, and I can hear it in her voice: she's lying.

CHAPTER SEVEN
KAITLIN

THERE'S A KEY CLUTCHED IN MY HAND, MASCARA RUN-
ning all over my face.

I'm a mess. A fucking mess! I hate crying. The first time I
killed somebody, I didn't cry. None of the times I've killed
people have tears been part of the equation. You might say
there's something wrong with me, and you'd probably be
right. But maybe there's nothing wrong with me, and you're
the one with the problem. Because emotions are weakness,
you know? Emotions are dirty, disgusting things.

You know what I like even less than emotions? Inconven-
ience. Like, right now I should be sitting down with Paddy,
since I haven't seen the old man in a year and he's the only
person I really care about impressing. Or, if he's busy, I'd be
getting my pussy eaten by one of his guys at the bar. I have
needs, and they don't discriminate particularly much. So

walking through the streets of Manhattan looking like a freak has me wishing death upon several people. Most of all, Theo and Sal Barbieri. It didn't take me too long to figure out who they were. Conniving little shitfucks. Especially since Ray, my father's driver, has been picking me up from the airport and fucking me in secret since I was fourteen.

You grow up quick in the McLaughlin family.

But more than even Theo and Sal, who I'd really like to get my hands on and strangle is Gracie fucking O'Connor. That cunt was meant to be guarding me – so that, you know, I don't have to be on alert – and she's a dead woman the next time I see her. She's fucking dead. It's always bothered me that Daddy liked Gracie, took her in, kept her in New York while he sent me away. He said I was going to Los Angeles for my own protection after what happened with the Barbieris, but he never brought me back. Kept stringing things out, let me come home once a year to see the family for summer break, but apart from that, I've been stuck in a smoggy, palm-tree lined desert for five fucking years. This time, I have no intentions of going back. I'm done. I'm coming back to New York, and I don't care what Paddy or Gracie or anyone says. If the Barbieris want me dead, well, I'll make sure every single one of *them* is dead before I make my return permanent. Even if I have to kill them myself.

Which is why the fact someone has just tried to kidnap me is utterly ridiculous. I know exactly who they are, *Jerry* and *Gareth*, those smug assholes who thought they could just take Gracie and I captive as easily as that. Theodore and Salvatore. I should have recognized them the second I slid my ass into that car. I'm an idiot! They're the reason I can't live in my own fucking town. They're the reason my life is the way it is. I don't care how irresistible they are, how much I want to have them both fuck me at the same time. I'm going to take great pleasure in wiping those two Barbieri brothers off the face of the earth.

But first, I need to get out of dodge. I need to get to a safe place before somebody sees me and plants a slug in my pretty blonde head. That chick back at the diner gave me her address and a key, and I'm really, really surprised that she did. But so she should have. If she hadn't, I would have told my father to cut her head off. People should know their place in this city.

People should fucking bow down to me.

But they don't, because it's 2015 and nobody fucking bows, and because I'm never here. Plus they're too scared. Pathetic, frightened creatures that walk along these streets like sheep, milling about in their meaningless lives, trying to pretend that this city isn't run by us.

It's so fucking hot I feel like I'm going to melt into the pavement and disappear before I can get to where I'm going. That chick's directions weren't too shoddy, and eventually I find myself standing in front of a crumbling apartment building that looks like it should be somewhere to shoot up or store dead bodies. It looks decrepit.

Well, beggars can't be choosers. I'm going to go inside, find this apartment, and find a phone to call my father to come get me out of this mess. And kill Gracie. And kill Theo and Sal. Probably not in that order, but it's close.

I scan the yellowed directory in the lobby that has each floor printed on it in fading letters. Looks like apartment six is on the sixth floor. Huh. It must be a floor per apartment. This place might be better than it looks if you get a whole floor to yourself.

I press the button for the lift, and wait. And wait. And wait. The front door to the building creaks open and I freak, rushing over to the stairs and talking them two at a time. I'm fit, I work out, I can take these stairs. More importantly, I don't need anyone to see me.

I really wish I had a fucking weapon right now.

On the sixth floor stairwell, I yank the heavy fire escape door open and enter a small landing, barely big enough for me to stand in, another door in front of me marked with a six. Weird-ass old buildings. I shove the key the diner girl gave me into the lock and turn it, but nothing happens. Fuck. This is apartment six, and this is the right address. I'm certain I haven't misunderstood anything.

I try to pull the key back out. It's stuck.

Jesus Christ. This day is going from bad to worse. When I'm done here, I'm going to burn down Cucino Diavola , snort a whole bunch of coke, and probably fuck Ray in the back of his limo while I watch the flames devour the Barbieriss.

One can only hope.

I'm trying to jiggle the key in the lock when the door flies open, and I stumble, letting go of the key as it's wrenched away. I'm immediately suspicious, but this is the right apartment—apartment six, like the key says—and this guy looks harmless enough.

I still wish I had a gun right about now, but Gracie always fucking takes mine away when we're flying. Says I'm too eager to shoot somebody to be trusted on a plane with a loaded weapon. She kind of has a point. I still fucking hate her, though.

The guy looks about thirty, six foot, his brown eyes intense and kind of weird-looking, like he's permanently squinting, even when he's not. He's wearing a checked shirt and sporting three days worth of facial hair – which is a shame, because if he tidied himself up, he'd be fucking hot, even with the serious-frowny-eyes thing he's got going on. But right now, he just looks... below average. I guess above average people don't live in falling-down, piece of shit apartment buildings like this.

I plaster on a smile as I look past him to the apartment within. The chick never mentioned someone being in her apartment, but I'm not worried. The years Gracie has spent teaching me self defense are something I always keep in my back pocket, and besides, this guy looks like an average Joe.

"Can I help you, sweetheart?" he asks, leaning one shoulder against the door frame as he looks me up and down in a similar fashion.

"I'm a friend of Scarlett's," I say, thankful I remembered the bitch's name. "She said I could hang here until she gets back."

Something flashes in the dude's eyes. Lust, pure and simple. I smirk at him. I tend to have that effect on men.

"Well come in," he says. "Any friend of Scarlett's is a friend of mine."

I step into the apartment, feeling relieved as the door shuts behind me.

Ten minutes later, I'm sitting at a small table that's designed for playing cards, wedged in the middle of a very small kitchen. This place is practically a fucking postage stamp, and I'm starting to itch, like I need some wide open space, but I need to wait.

I've since learned that the guy who answered the door, the one now sitting across from me, is called Jimmy, and the one to my right is his younger brother, Dave. Jimmy's a building super, he tells me, and works part-time at a hospital. Dave, who is basically just a baby-faced, clean-shaven version of his brother, also works at the hospital. Oh, and he's a magician in his spare time.

A.Fucking.Magician.

"Do you mind if I borrow your cell phone?" I ask Jimmy, fluttering my eyelashes at him as Dave shuffles a deck of cards beside me. I'm well aware that I need to get the fuck out of dodge, but I also need to be polite. I hate people – I'd rather just fucking do what I want to do – but there are social rules I need to follow in order to get what I want. I've finally learned this, after eighteen years of being a loose fucking cannon. I can't afford to be like that if I want to come back to New York on a permanent basis. Discretion and bullshit artistry are my new lucky charms, my way of getting ahead in this family business of mine before someone like Gracie comes along and steals my fucking spoils.

"It's charging," Jimmy says. "Give it a couple minutes and it should have enough juice to make a call."

"Thanks," I say, dazzling him with a smile full of my perfect teeth. *All the better to eat you with,* I think as I tilt my head to the side, studying Jimmy openly. He's kind of hot in a lazy way, and I'm fucking horny. I finish my evaluation as I'm thrumming my long red nails against the plastic card table. *Nah. Not fuckable enough for Kaitlin McLaughlin. Sorry, buddy.*

"So how'd you say you knew Scarlett again?" Jimmy asks, as he cuts a lime into segments and wedges one piece into his bottle of beer. He repeats the action with two more beers, sliding one in front of his brother and the other over to me. I take the beer with a smile of thanks, popping the lime inside the bottle with my index finger and taking a gulp. A slow smile spreads across Jimmy's face as he watches me swallow, and I can tell he wants to get into my pants. Or my mouth. Or both.

"We're just friends," I shrug, feeling irritated that I have to explain myself to these guys. Why the fuck should I have to?

"And she told you to come to Jimmy's apartment?" Dave chimes in, laughing. "That's hilarious. I thought for sure that Scar fucking hated Jimmy." He punches his brother in the arm, but Jimmy doesn't move. He's not smiling at all now, his tongue sliding over his teeth as he stares at me with zero expression.

I look down at the key in front of me, sitting innocently next to the beer bottle. There used to be a line on top of the six, but it's mostly faded away. And it's then I realize. The number written on the card isn't a six.

It's a nine.

It used to be underlined so you could tell the difference, but it's so scuffed and faded, you could easily read it as either a six or a nine.

Dave sees me glance at the key tag, his lips stretching into a grin that bares his teeth. He's not dangerous looking, not really. Neither of them is. But it doesn't matter. They're wolves, just like me. I see this now. I see it all; the way they've positioned themselves, in between me and the front door. The casual way Jimmy keeps his hand on his knife. *This is the wrong apartment.*

Dave picks the key up, his deck of cards forgotten. I glance over at Jimmy, whose eyes are looking rather psychotic right now. I don't move as he takes the knife and points it at me across the tiny card table, pressing the sharp tip against the bare flesh between my tits. I'm having a hard time staying still, though; I'm suddenly dizzy, and this tiny room feels like it's about to crush me. I take a deep breath, looking at the bottle of beer in front me, my vision doubling as it becomes two bottles. *Fuck.*

"You drugged me," I slur, fighting to hold onto the table, but I'm slipping.

"You should really replace these keys, bro," Dave says, taking the key tag between his thumb and forefinger and turning it upside down - no, turning it the right way - so it says 9. Apartment nine. Fuck. *I've been in the wrong apartment this entire time.* I lose my balance, Jimmy's knife nicking my skin as I slide off my chair and hit the kitchen floor with a solid whack. I see stars for a moment, rolling onto my back as I take rapid breaths of air into my lungs. There's a blackness that wants to descend upon me, and my body wants to let it smother me to sleep. No. Fuck that. *Stay awake, Kaitlin.* Stay the fuck awake.

Jimmy stands over me so he's got one foot on either side of my waist. He looks down at me, sporting a grave expression as he cocks his head to one side.

My eyes flutter rapidly, trying to stay open despite the drug that's filtering through my bloodstream right now. I should have known. It was all too fucking easy. "You... work for Barbieri?" I ask nobody in particular, my tongue feeling like it's filling my entire mouth.

Dave appears in my vision, standing next to his brother, his face crumpled up in confusion. "Who the fuck is Barbieri? We don't work for nobody, sweetheart. We just know a good opportunity when we see one."

I see the tug of a smile at the side of Jimmy's hard-set mouth, and then I'm fucking *gone.*

CHAPTER EIGHT
JASE

WE'RE RUNNING.

Julz sits across from me, fixing her long brown hair up in a messy top-knot. She sees me looking at her and gives me a tight smile, a smile that says she's freaking out as much as I am.

We weren't in Colorado a year before the cartel caught up with us. The cartel run by my father's family in his absence, the absence created when Juliette shot him dead. It's strange how naïve we were back then, how we thought that killing my father would solve everything.

And now, sitting in the back of a limo we hailed at the airport, an hour after we've touched down in New York, it's starting to sink in just how much danger we're still in.

The limo pulls into the kerb and glides to a halt, the sound of the bustling city outside almost too much for me to handle.

I'm fucking angry that we're here, fucking angry that we've had to leave our home, fucking angry that we've had to leave our daughter's grave behind. The thought of the Cartel or the Gypsy Brothers defacing her headstone fills my veins with so much hate, it's a wonder my blood doesn't run black.

"We're here," Julz says somberly, peering through the heavily-tinted limo window at the apartment building Elliot's directed us to. We're here in a holding pattern, waiting for new fake passports and bank accounts to come through before we find a more permanent bolt-hole. We thought we'd wait it out in Colorado, figured we'd have enough time up our sleeve before they found us.

We were wrong.

I pay the driver and grab our bags out of the trunk. There isn't much, because there was no time to pack much before the warning call came through. A motorcade of slick black cars, flanked by motorcycles, speeding towards us as we slept. Motherfuckers didn't even try to be subtle about it.

A chartered flight was waiting for us at the airport thanks to generous friends, and Elliot's arranged somewhere for us to crash for the night, although I doubt I'll do any sleeping. There's every chance those motherfuckers followed us, and we can never be too careful. It's become the way we live. It's fraught with tension.

It's exhausting.

At least we're not dead, I reason to myself. Almost on cue, a painful twinge sparks in my chest, a reminder that some things can never be truly forgotten. When Dornan Ross, my own fucking father, shot me in the chest, I was almost dead. I pulled through, and I'm fine now, but the doctors tell me they'll never be able to pull all the tiny fragments of the shattered bullet from my chest, no matter how many times they try. So now I carry them with me, a lasting mark of his hate, the same way Juliette carries her own scars from him.

The pain's not necessarily a bad thing for me, though. It's a reminder. We won. We fucking won, and I got my girl back. My Juliette.

My chest hurts a little less at that thought.

We enter the apartment building we've been directed to and head up the stairs to the ninth floor, automatically bypassing the lift. Sure, we could get cornered in a stairwell just as easily as a lift, but the stairs feel safer. There's a key shoved in a dying pot plant by the door, very subtle.

Once we're in the apartment, I dump our bags in the middle of the floor and take my gun from my waistband, making sure the space is clear. It takes me all of five seconds. The place is a studio apartment, and for a moment I wonder where we're going to sleep. Maybe the chick who lives here is staying somewhere else at Elliot's request. I make a mental note to call him and find out what the deal is, but first, I need to chill for a minute, regroup. It all happened so quickly last night, the harried phone call telling us to get out, the frantic packing of the few things truly valuable to us. We don't have much, because we've never had much, but we have a couple bags full of cash, plenty of credit cards in false names, and most importantly, *we have each other*. After I'm satisfied nobody is lurking in the closet or the bathroom, the only two places a person could reasonably hide, I tuck my gun back into my jeans and automatically reach for Julz. She's gained a few pounds, looks much healthier now. There was a time when I was terrified she was going to fade away into nothing, into skin and bone. But she's back. My Juliette is back, more beautiful than ever.

"I'm gonna pass out if I don't take some layers off," she says, pulling back from me and gesturing to her long sleeves and jeans. I'm the same, so hot I feel like my skull could explode. It was freezing cold when we left Colorado in the dead of the night, but New York is the polar opposite, muggy and still. I take another step back and take my hoodie off, watching as Juliette shimmies out of her jeans. A moment later, she's wearing nothing except a sheer pair of panties and a gauzy, ivory-colored bra that leaves very, very little to my imagination.

Just watching her undress makes my cock hard, my eyes taking in every inch of her body as I shift slightly on my feet. She grabs a shirt from her bag and shakes it out, going to put it over her head. At the last minute I catch her wrist, a devious smile spreading across my face. She looks at my hand around her wrist, and then up at my face. I can already see her nipples peaking to hard points through her gauzy white bra, and my mouth waters in anticipation.

"Jason," she cautions, but her tone is playful. Daring, almost.

"Juliette," I reply. My dick is as hard as a rock, and all I want to do is sink it into her soft, wet pussy.

I tug on her wrist, pulling her closer so her straining tits are pressed up against my chest. I lean down and dart my tongue out, feeling her squirm as I lick over the thin material covering her nipple. I straighten again, sucking at the sensitive flesh at her neck as she writhes against my grip.

"We're in somebody's house," she protests weakly. I ignore her, running one of my hands down her hip and into her sheer panties, my fingers finding her hard nub. "She's not coming back until tonight," I murmur, swirling my finger against her clit as I take her mouth with mine and kiss her roughly. She moans against my lips, and it takes every ounce of my will-power not to throw her against the couch and fuck her into oblivion.

I push further into her panties, my fingers finding her already wet for me. Un-fucking-believable. My dick is begging for release, especially with the new knowledge that Juliette is dripping wet and ready for me. I'm about to slide my fingers into her wetness when she pulls her wrist away and reaches for the hem of my shirt, pulling it up and over my head. Sweat glistens on my chest as she peels the cotton away from my skin—this city is as hot as a fucking furnace—but instead of trying to avoid it, she slides her hand down the middle of my slick chest as I slow-thrust two fingers into her soaking pussy.

She throws her head back, groaning my name. Jesus Christ. I'll never get sick of hearing that on her mouth, of worshipping her body. I'm always careful with her, after everything that's happened, never let myself go unless she begs me for it first. I like to fuck her hard and fast and brutal, but she has to ask for it first. Those are our rules. It doesn't work any other way. In the beginning, after we'd first arrived in Colorado, I couldn't even touch her, knowing all the things that had happened. The horrible, unspeakable things my father had done to her, all the ways he'd broken and scarred her, body and soul. It took us a long time to know each other again, to be able to trust. It took me a long time to trust m*yself* around her, knowing the kind of man my father was. His dark legacy haunts me, but now, I finally feel like we're starting to move away from the past and create something new, something that belongs only to us.

"Couch," she says, the need in her voice irresistible. "Sit. Now."

I slide my fingers from her and undo my jeans, using my free hand to pull my gun from my waistband and toss it on the small coffee table next to the couch. I do as I'm told, taking a step back and sitting on the couch, my dick straining against my boxers. I take it in my palm and coat it with her wetness, pumping with my hand a few times. Even that motion makes me want to come right now, but I know that this is only going to get better. Hotter. Wetter.

"Close your eyes," Juliette says. Oh, fuck. I make sure the gun's in easy reach and the front door in my line of sight, and then I allow my eyes to close. For a few seconds there's nothing, and I wonder what she's doing.

And then *her sweet fucking mouth is on my dick.*

Fuuuuuuuuck.

My balls protest, demanding I shoot my load onto her tongue right this second, but I'm more controlled than that. I open my eyes, moaning a small sigh of appreciation as I thread my hands into her long hair. She swirls her tongue over the swollen head of my cock before taking me all the way into her throat. Goddamn, I want to come. I want to fuck her sweet mouth until I explode inside it.

But I don't want to come yet. I'm not ready for this to be over, no way. She seems to read my mind, taking her mouth away and sitting back on her heels. My initial disappointment at the sudden loss of her lips sucking at my dick is quickly replaced by excitement, as she crawls into my lap and straddles me. I couldn't give a flying fuck that we're doing this in somebody else's apartment, on their couch. Nope. *Sorry, gracious person who said we could hide out here for the night. I'm about to fuck this beautiful girl right in the middle of your apartment, and I'm going to make her scream.*

Julz arranges herself in my lap, her underwear still on. The sight of her pussy, covered by her sheer panties, only drives me more wild. I've got a thing for fucking with clothes on. Somehow it feels better, knowing that she can be standing there in a dress and panties one minute, getting on with her day, and bent over a table with my dick in her ass the next.

I rest my hands at my sides, wanting nothing more than to grab her hips and slam her down onto my waiting cock, but I don't. I enjoy the anticipation, the thrill of waiting for her to pleasure herself with me.

I'm fucking panting, waiting for her to make a move, and she does, leaning forward and kissing me full on the mouth. At the same time, I feel her lace-covered pussy grind against my cock, and I buck my hips up in response.

"Are you ready?" she asks, teasing me as she nibbles at my lips. I sit further back, sinking into the couch as my cock juts up in my lap, pointing at what I want. At where I want to be.

Balls-deep inside her.

Yeah.

"Julz, baby," I groan, taking a handful of her hair and clutching it in one fist. "I was born ready."

She smiles knowingly, her fingers down at her panties, and I look down to see her pulling aside the scrap of material that's stopping me from driving into her like a fucking freight train. She positions her hips forward slightly, and then she sinks.Down.On.My.Cock.

I have to fight not to come inside her as soon as her slick walls are squeezing me tight. For a moment, I can't breathe, I can't think. All I can do is let my eyes shut, and tense to stop my dick from coating the inside of her warm pussy with my load.

"Fuck me," she whispers, her face scrunching up in pleasure. I don't need to be told twice. I take hold of her hips, lifting her up so only the head of my cock is still inside her, before slamming her down into my lap. A few of those and she starts to tighten around me, throwing her head back as her eyes close. "Don't stop, don't stop, don't stop!" she moans, her nails digging into my shoulders as her pussy walls contract tightly around my dick, pulsing, bringing me dangerously close to the edge. I resist the urge to come with her, because I know she'll keep coming all morning if I play my cards right. And really, it's not like we can sightsee, because we're being fucking hunted, so I might as well have her whispering my name as she comes all afternoon, too.

Sated, she lets her head fall forward on my shoulder, her

limbs like putty. She drapes herself over me, her tits crushed against my chest, hugging me tightly. I wrap my arms around her, hugging her back. I love this woman more than anything on this earth. I'd fucking die and go to hell for her, and I still have to pinch myself to believe she's all mine.

She starts rocking her hips again, slowly, little whimpers coming from her. She gets super sensitive after she comes, and every tiny movement must be driving her crazy. "I want you to finish in my mouth," she whispers, and just the sound of her words nearly drives me over the edge. Holy fuck, it's like she can read my mind and knows exactly what to do to get me off.

"You better get your mouth down there then," I manage to say, lifting her hips so she can get off my cock. "I'm *this* fucking close."

I watch with an insatiable desire as she climbs back between my legs and takes my rock-hard dick into her mouth. She loosens her jaw, letting me slide deep down into her tight throat. I fist two hands in her hair, because I can't fucking resist anymore, and my whole body tenses as my cock pumps come into her mouth. She doesn't pull away until I'm finished, and only then does she take her mouth away and smile. And then she *swallows*. Sweet Jesus, what did I do to deserve her? She's perfect. Fucking perfect. She only came once though, and that's not good enough for me.

"You want to come again, baby?" I ask her. She grins, nodding. I take her wrists and pull her up so she's straddling me again, only this time I slide down the couch between her legs, bracing my knees against the floor as my mouth lines up with her pussy. It's plump and pink, like it's just been fucked. And I'm not finished yet.

"Hold on to the back of the couch," I instruct, and she does. I know she wants this. I can tell by the way she's breathing heavily, by how soaking wet her pussy still is.

I grab the round globes of her ass and pull her into me, so my tongue can grind against her clit. She shudders, almost losing her balance. "Hold on tight," I growl, darting my tongue against her again.

"Oh, fuck," she cries, as I stick two fingers inside her wet heat again.

"That's right," I say, pumping my fingers. "Move your hips. Fuck my face, baby."

She comes again, all over my tongue and my fingers, and it's fucking beautiful. Afterwards, I slide back up through her legs, and she folds herself into my arms. We're both exhausted. I glance at the radio clock on the wall. It's not even midday yet.

"I've never been to New York," she murmurs into my chest. I stroke her hair, that anxious, angry feeling in my chest returning as the post-sex euphoria slowly fades away. "Me either," I reply, pressing my lips to the top of her head.

My phone rings, almost as if on cue. I search in my jeans pockets—I never even got to take them off—and locate my phone, dragging it out and looking at the screen.

Elliot. Fuck. I gotta answer this.

"Hey, man, what's up?" I ask, clearing my throat.

"Did you find the place okay?" he asks. Juliette slides off my lap and starts picking up pieces of clothing, while I watch her ass with great interest.

"Yeah," I say, more than a little distracted. "Hey, thanks for organizing it so quickly. What time did you say your cousin was due back?" *How many hours do I have left to make Juliette come for me?*

"Scarlett does a double shift today," Elliot says. "She said she'd be back around six."

I smile to myself. That's almost a full day, trapped in this apartment together.

I can't think of anything better. If we keep ourselves occupied, maybe, just maybe, I can drive my demons and hers away, at least until tomorrow.

CHAPTER NINE
SAL

"You told me to leave you here," I say to Katya, tossing the spare length of rope on the floor.

"I thought you were going to get me Starbucks!" she screams, her face flush as the vibrator continues its magic. I make a mental note to check the brand of batteries powering that thing.

"Please, Sal," Katya moans. "Please take it out. It won't stop. I've been coming all morning and *I can't get it out.*"

Now, normally that shit would get me harder than the steel my gun is made out of. But right now, I'm freaking the fuck out.

"Oh, now *she's* coming," Scarlett says, looking sulky as fuck tied to my chair. *Hot as fuck,* but sulky as fuck. I run my hand through my hair, my brother's voice telling me to get a fucking haircut ringing in my ears as I hear my ringtone again.

Dun dun dundundundun dundundun ...

About to lose my shit and shoot everyone in the room—and then myself—I rip the phone from my pants pocket and hit answer.

"What?!" I snap.

"Where the fuck have you been?!" Theo growls down the line, making me want to reach through the phone and punch him in the fucking face. Where have I been? Where has *he* been? He was meant to bag the bodyguard and then follow me to Kaitlin. The rational part of me knows he's in his own world of trouble right now, but I have a bad habit of being defensive when he drills me. Which he does every goddamn day. *Cut your hair, Sal. Turn this shitty music off, Sal. Change your ringtone, Sal.* Shit. Maybe I should set the mopey bastard up with Scarlett. They could talk about their mutual hatred of my music choices while I bash their heads together.

Or maybe they can all just suck my dick, because I'm tired and hung over as fuck, and I'm pretty sure that smell is from Katya pissing in my bed.

"I've been busy," I say calmly. The rage that burns inside my chest is punctuated by my brother's heavy breathing, Scarlett's insolent stare, Katya's sexual pleadings and the moaning of two porn stars on the fifty-inch screen that hangs on my bedroom wall.

"Are you ... *screwing* someone right now?" Theo asks, his voice rising with each word until he's yelling. "Are you screwing *Kaitlin* right now?!"

I grind my teeth together as I raise my gun and shoot the

fucking TV. It explodes in an impressive shower of sparks and glass. That's gonna be a bitch for my cleaner to get out of the carpet.

"No," I say. "I'm not."

Katya starts moaning, tipping her head back as she widens her legs, her shaved pussy soaking wet as it contracts around the buzzing vibrator I jammed in there several hours ago.

"I'm coming again!" Katya moans, her breathing loud and uneven as her eyes roll back in her dumb head. She looks like she's having more fun than me right now, though. My head feels like it's gonna fucking explode, just like the TV screen.

"Sal ..." Theo growls.

"Hang on," I say tightly, hitting the mute button and setting the phone down on my nightstand. I stalk into my bathroom, grabbing a hand towel from the neat pile my maid has arranged for me. Returning to the bedroom, I avoid Scarlett's stare as I reach between Katya's legs and pull out the vibrator. It makes a wet slurping noise as it comes out, and I grimace as I use another part of the towel to switch the thing off, tossing it in the trash basket in my bathroom.

Katya pants heavily, looking at me through far too much mascara and smudged eyeliner. Her red lipstick is smeared across her face, and I thank Christ that I had a good long shower this morning and scrubbed the bright red rings off my cock.

Colorstay lipstick is hot, but not when it won't wash off your balls.

I clear my throat awkwardly as I start undoing the ropes that secure Katya to my massive bed. She's been spread-eagled for at least two hours, maybe more. I mean, I left her here, went to the restaurant, got the car sorted with Theo, picked up those Irish bitches, totalled the car (thanks Theo), lost the girls, found Scarlett, and carjacked a cab driver.

And all the while, Katya was having orgasms tied to my bed. *Poor thing*, I think sarcastically. Wish I could switch my fucking morning with hers. Multiple orgasms doesn't sound too shoddy right now, faced with the very real possibility that I might be dead by nightfall.

I think of last night, of coming down Katya's throat and all over her face, my dick a little sad that it might not ever fuck again. Since, you know, I'll be buried in Bleecker Gardens in a couple hours at the rate things are going.

"I can't believe you left me here," Katya says.

I raise my eyebrows at her. "You told me to leave you here."

"I thought you were running to Starbucks!" she repeats.

"You should really get her a latte or something," Scarlett pipes up from her spot in the corner. "Caffeine withdrawal is a bitch."

"Yeah," I say, undoing the last knot on Katya's ankle. "Almost as bad as alcohol withdrawal, right?"

Her mouth forms a tight line, and I can tell I've pissed her off.

Good.

Dun dun dundundundun dundundun ...

Fuck! Theo's hung up and re-dialled. I snatch the phone up, answering it again. "I'm dealing with a fucking situation here!" I yell.

"You leave the phone *now?*" Theo screeches, so loud I have

to pull the phone away from my ear. Out of the corner of my eye, I can see Katya pulling her clothes on. I suppose she doesn't want to stick around and shower, since I've just tied a chick up and shot a TV screen in front of her.

I can't say I blame her.

"I'm a little busy!" I say to my brother.

"Have you got Kaitlin?" he asks impatiently.

"No," I reply. "But I have someone who knows where she is." I look at Scarlett, who appears bored, annoyed and amused all at the same time. One thing she doesn't appear is scared, and that unsettles me greatly. She's cool as a mother-fucking cucumber.

"Who?" Theo demands. I hear a loud crash.

"Some chick who's hiding her," I explain. "Bro, have you got the bodyguard under control?"

"Yeah," Theo huffs. I hear another crash.

"I gotta go," Theo says breathlessly. "Answer your fucking phone next time."

He ends the call, and I stare at the screen for a moment, debating whether I should shoot it or not. Taking a deep breath, I shove the phone in my pocket. It can live, for now.

"Are you going to fuck her?" Katya says, her eyes narrowed. The phone call forgotten, I snap to my senses just in time to see Katya dressed and looming over Scarlett. Who, to her credit, looks entirely unperturbed by the tall, blonde Russian chick with murder in her eyes.

I rush over, push her away from Scarlett and hand her her shoes. "I'm going to torture her, and then I'm probably going to shoot her and bury her out back. If you're jealous, Katya, pull up a fucking seat and I'll do the same to you."

She swallows thickly, glances at Scarlett one last time, and backs slowly out of the room. A few moments later, I hear my front door slam.

"You said you weren't going to shoot me," Scarlett says.

I ball my fists up. "I'm not."

She's quiet for a beat. Then, "I think that chick pissed the bed."

I'm gonna smash something. Scarlett's face is too pretty, and if I wasn't so wound up I'd probably be crying my Italian ass off laughing at her inane comments, but right now? I need to smash something.

"It could be worse," Scarlett says, clearly goading me. "At least she didn't shit the bed."

CHAPTER TEN
THEO

I KNOW EXACTLY WHERE TO FIND MY FATHER. WHEN he's at Cucina Diavolo, he's always in the small study he keeps on the ground floor, usually with a glass of whiskey in his hand and a frown cutting into the brutal lines of his narrow face. Today is no exception. Wallace, his longest-serving and only friend is with him, staring out of the tiny window that overlooks the herb garden outside in the courtyard. When he sees me, Wallace nods his head in my father's general direction and goes to leave.

"Stick around, Wally," my father says, stopping him in his tracks. "I want you to tell my son here what's been happening this morning."

My stomach lurches. Shandi said Roberto wanted to see me, but she didn't say what about. I assumed it was because of Kaitlin. Sal and I were meant to bring the girl right back here and we haven't. And my brother isn't here, either, so the old man is going to know something's up. He casts sharp eyes over me, and, as if he just read my mind, says, "Where's your brother, Theo?"

"He's with the girl. We split up. We ran into a few … *complications.*"

My father looks at me like I'm something he just scraped off his shoe. "I think I know a little about your complications, son. Come. Walk with me. You too, Wallace. I need to eat something before the whiskey goes to my head."

Not even midday and Roberto's half buzzed. Nothing new. Ever since our mother died, this is how he's been. And no one fucking dares say a word to him about it, either. It wouldn't be worth their lives.

He stands, still gripping hold of his whiskey tumbler, and stalks out of the study, heading for the kitchen. Wallace and I are expected to follow, and so we dutifully do so, me ahead of the older, grey-haired guy. There are even more people in the kitchen than there were when I dragged Gracie through here earlier. With the old man's birthday celebrations at the restaurant tonight, there are more prep guys bringing in fresh ingredients and working furiously at the stations, but there are also three of my father's handymen standing by the fryers, apparently waiting for him. In between them, they're holding onto a bookie, Sammy Preston, a guy with the worst luck in the world. He started running books because he's good at math but terrible at the actual gambling part. Told me once he figured he'd cut his losses and make himself some cash off other people throwing theirs away instead of the other way around. He's visibly sweating as we cross the kitchen, and I have a sudden and overwhelmingly bad feeling about what he's doing here.

"Sammy," my father says, clapping him on the shoulder. "Thanks for coming by. I heard you had some interesting visitors at your place earlier this morning?"

"Cops," Sammy says, nodding like crazy. "Some kid got shot on my street or something. They wanted to know if I'd seen anything. I said no, of course." His words run together, betraying his nerves and also the fact that he's lying. It sounds too practiced, too plotted out to be the truth. My father knows this.

"I heard different, Sammy. And I hate hearing shit like this. It really ruins my day. See, how I heard it was like this. My friend down at the Midtown precinct calls me and lets me know that Fox Five News are running chopper footage of a car crash that took place on the George Washington Bridge," he casts a sideways glance at me and I know I'm fucking done for, "and he says there's this close-up shot of a guy that looks just like my kid fighting with a *woman*, and he's getting his ass kicked." Again, another cool, hard look at me. "And then, my friend at the Midtown precinct, he tells me that one of their detectives has received a call from one of their informants, letting them know that the guy on the bridge getting his ass kicked by a woman is in fact my son, Theo Barbieri. And then do you know what he said?" my father asks. He picks up a piece of cherry tomato one of the chefs is preparing and tosses it into his mouth. Shooing the chef away, he picks up the guy's knife and begins slicing the tomatoes himself.

Sammy looks around the gathering of men, as though he's waiting to see if he's actually supposed to respond. What he needs to do is keep his mouth shut, but even that won't help him now. If he's been informing to the cops, and if he called and informed them *I* was the guy on that bridge, then he's dead and nothing he can do or say is going to save him.

Roberto looks up at me from underneath drawn brows, scowling. "Where's your brother, Theo?"

"With the girl. They were headed to his place. I drew off the police."

My father hammers the knife he's holding into the chopping board without looking, the sound like machine gun fire. Perfectly even, sliced tomato stacks up while I start to sweat almost as badly as Sammy. "I saw your little circus performance shortly after my phone call ended. Can you guess what was going through my head at the time, Theo?"

"That your son really knows how to roll the fuck out of a car?"

Roberto points the knife at me and growls. "Shut your smart mouth."

I do, because my father doesn't tell you twice. He turns around and clears his throat, leaning against the counter, studying a now very, very anxious Sammy. My father tosses more tomato into his mouth, chewing thoroughly before saying, "My friend tells me that Sammy Preston, the bookie I use to run my own fucking gambling ring, is the guy who's informing on my son. I thought to myself, now how can that be? That makes no sense. But sure enough, when I look into it, I find out that it's true. That you have been giving the police information for the past six months."

"No! No, I would never—" Sammy, poor bastard, doesn't get to finish denying that this is true. My father nods to one of the men, Alfie, who then grabs Sammy by the back of the neck and shoves him down. It all happens so quickly. One minute the guy's standing there with a look of horror on his face, then the next his fucking head is in the deep fryer and his body is shaking so violently that the other two men have to hold him up.

My father folds his arms across his chest and watches as Sammy the bookie becomes Sammy the late bookie. I can hear my blood roaring in my ears. I've seen some pretty gnarly stuff before, especially at the hands of my father, but when Sammy stops moving and they let go of his body I know shit's hit a new level of fucked up. Sammy's entire head looks like it's been melted. His mouth gapes open, his eyelids, his actual *eyeballs* just fucking *gone*, and I turn around and throw up onto the polished tiles of the kitchen.

My ears are ringing.

I feel contact on my back—my father's hand. When I straighten up, he's watching me with a look of disappointment on his face that I should be used to by now. "Did you call the specialist like I asked you to?"

"We did. He wasn't interested," I say. "He didn't want to speak to us."

Roberto grunts. "And where is your brother, Theo?" This is the third time he's asked me that question. He obviously hasn't liked my response the first two times. I wipe my mouth with the back of my hand, gasping for breath. I know the only response that will please Roberto is, *he's right here, waiting for you.* "I'll get him. I'll bring him here," I say. Roberto nods, smiling sadly, like I've finally just understood and, boy, is it hard work being my father. He casually lifts the knife from the countertop and holds it against my throat. I can feel its cruel edge biting into my skin. For a second I think he's going to do it; I think he's actually going to cut my throat.

"I want you back in an hour," he tells me quietly. "I want both my children standing in front of me where I can see them. And I want that Irish bitch on her knees in front of me. Do you understand?"

"Yes, sir."

"Off you go."

I back away from the knife; my blood marks the steel, bright red as I step away from him. I try not to look at dead Sammy's mangled head but macabre fascination draws my eyes to the floor against my will. My stomach rolls again, ready to purge whatever's left inside it. I have got to get the fuck out of here before that happens again. The last thing I need is to disgust Roberto even further. Have him change his mind about the pressure he wants to apply with that knife of his.

As soon as I'm out of the kitchen, I pull out my phone and call Sal. Motherfucker had better pick up this time. I can*not* fucking handle our father on my own. I have to know if he's even fucking found—

"*What?!*" Sal's voice on the other end of the phone sounds seriously pissed off. I'll give him fucking what.

"Where the fuck have you been?"

There's a long pause before my brother exhales and says, "I've been busy." He sounds like he's kicking back, relaxing, not a worry in the world. I could kill the motherfucker. My anger levels spike when I hear something in the background. Something very, *very* bad. I pause a second, listening hard, making sure my ears aren't playing tricks on me. But nope. I can hear moaning.

"Are you ... *are you screwing someone right now?* Are you screwing Kaitlin?"

"No. I am not."

"*I'm coming again!*" a female voice moans in the background. This is ridiculous. Absolutely fucked. I've just been subjected to someone getting their head fucking deep fried and my brother is out somewhere sticking his dick inside our hostage. I'm going to castrate him.

"Sal—"

"Hang on." The line goes dead. Not dead, but silent, like I'm on hold. Now is not a good time to be putting me on hold. I am about to seriously lose my shit. I hang up the call and dial him again, cursing him out under my breath. When he picks up I scream at him.

He sounds pissed that I'm pissed, and I want to reach down the goddamn phone and strangle him. "Have you got Kaitlin?" I snap.

"No. But I have someone who knows where she is."

This is not what I wanted to hear from him. Not even close. I grip hold of the phone, doing my best not to snap and throw the fucking thing. "Who?"

"Some chick who's hiding her. Bro, have you got the

bodyguard under control?"

"Yeah." The door to the kitchen opens and Alfie backs out into the hallway, dragging Sammy's dead body behind him. Alfie grunts at me, trips, and drops Sammy. His head hits the floor hard, cracking against the tiles. *Fuuuuuck.* "I gotta go," I say into the receiver. "Answer your fucking phone next time." I kill the connection, backing away down the hallway. I need to get the hell out of here right fucking now. Roberto said he wanted us back here in one hour. That's blatantly not going to happen since Sal doesn't have Kaitlin, so the best thing I can do is get my ass as far away from Cucina Diavolo as possible. Until we have that Irish princess, this is seriously not a safe place to be.

CHAPTER ELEVEN
SCARLETT

IT'S SAD, YOU KNOW, THAT THE THING THAT SPURS ME on to get out isn't the fact that I'm scared for my life.

Because I'm not scared, not really.

I honestly don't really give a fuck what happens to me.

And that realization is almost freeing.

The problem, though, is that even though I don't care, my body *does*. Very much so. Those little white pills that get me through the day are in my purse, and my purse is back at the diner. And I'm suddenly not feeling very good. I'm dizzy, I'm sweating, and I'm fairly sure if I don't get to a bathroom soon, I'm going to throw up all over Sal's plush carpet.

He's busy fussing with the sheets. He rips everything off the bed and disappears, his feet thudding down the stairs and back up again.

When he returns, he's got fresh sheets that he tosses on the bare mattress. He turns to me and frowns, as though he's deciding whether to go ahead and make the bed, or start going to town on me with a rusty screwdriver until I talk.

"Don't stop on my account," I say, a little slower than I would have liked. My mouth is so dry, and my heart is pounding. Fuck. I knew I should have taken one of those tablets before I started my shift, but usually the alcohol gives me enough of a buzz until mid-morning when I take my first pill.

Timing is everything when you're keeping yourself doped to the eyeballs day and night.

"I need to go to the bathroom," I mumble.

He shrugs. "Guess you'll just have to wait, sweetheart."

I glare at him. "You really want two chicks pissing in your room today?"

He clenches his jaw, looking unimpressed. He leaves me for a moment, going into his bathroom, and when he comes out, he's holding a large, very sharp cutthroat razor.

My eyes must wig out, because he smirks at me, placing the razor on top of the doorframe, where I'll never be able to reach it.

"Don't worry," he says. "I'm not going to use it."

He closes the space between us, untying my wrists. "Two minutes," he says.

I massage my wrists. They feel tender from where he tied the rope, but he didn't tie it very tight. It's just that my skin is so fucking sensitive right now, it's like paper-thin glass, ready to shatter into a million pieces and leave me a bleeding mess. At least, that's what it feels like when I can't get my pills and booze when I need it.

I nod, because I don't even have the energy to speak anymore. Sal raises an eyebrow, giving me a strange look, but I need to be sick. Now.

I've only gone through withdrawals once before. It was back when I'd just gotten here and my doctor back in LA had prescribed the Oxy to keep me functioning through the worst of the court shit. I guess he didn't want me jumping off a building like I kept threatening. The drugs numbed me, gave me some artificial sense of calm, a buzz in my stomach that I became rapidly obsessed with maintaining at all times.

Then he cut me off.

Fucker said I'd become too dependent on them and refused to prescribe them anymore. I'd been in New York three weeks by then, and I was tripping out.

Until I found Taylor, selling the shit at the AA meeting I'd been instructed to go to as part of my parole.

After that, it was just a matter of juggling enough tips to get my hands on a couple of the pills each day. Ideally I'd get more, but they were expensive, so I compensated by spacing out my doses and filling the voids with cheap alcohol. It's worked pretty well for the past seven months that I've been existing out here.

I lock the bathroom door behind me, holding my hair back as I retch over the toilet bowl. God, it's disgusting. I haven't eaten since last night, and all that comes up is coffee and the burning vodka I consumed earlier.

Losing the vodka to the toilet bowl makes me sad. Hopefully I got most of the alcohol in my bloodstream before that happened, because today's going to be a fucker. Then again, Sal might do me a favor and kill me.

"Hurry up," Sal yells, pounding twice on the door. I roll my eyes, flushing the toilet and rinsing my mouth out under the fancy tap. This guy's got to be rich, I think, because everything in this house stinks of money. Even the chick in his bed looked like an upmarket slut. I take a little bit of toothpaste from the tube on the counter and rub it around my teeth to get rid of the vomit taste, and then my eyes are scanning every square inch of the room, looking for a weapon.

I could squirt shampoo at him. Nope, too messy and difficult. He's taken the razor. Could I strangle him with a towel? Negatory. He'd strangle me with it. He seems to enjoy cutting off my air supply.

I'm coming up blank when my eyes settle on the toilet cistern, and more specifically, the heavy porcelain lid that covers it.

Excitedly, I grip each side with my fingers and pull up, testing the weight of the thick slab. I can definitely maneuver it.

Lucky I'm a fucking actress, I think. I let the lid slide back into place and then wash my hands in the sink. I dry them off before going back for some more water—not much, just a little sip that I hold with my tongue against the roof of my mouth. I unlock the bathroom door and pull it open to see Sal leaning against the doorframe.

"I hope you used air freshener," he says with a smirk. I don't respond, other than to put my hand to my mouth. *Game on, motherfucker.* I make my eyes go wide and rush back to the toilet, facing away from him and making a retching sound as I open my mouth, letting the water dribble out of my mouth and into the toilet.

I continue to make the most disgusting noises possible with my throat, resting a hand on the cistern.

Come on. Come on, Barbieri. Come and get me.

"Bet you're needing a drink right about now, you little vodka-soaked degenerate?"

I don't answer. I don't move. Come closer.

"Or maybe it's those little white pills I found in your purse. Yeah, I think that's what's got your panties in a twist. You've got the bends."

I resist the impulse to fire off a witty retort or my standard Fuck You. I clamp my mouth shut.

Closer, motherfucker.

"Sal," I say softly, looking up at him with my glassy eyes. Yeah, I can cry on demand as well.

"Cat got your tongue, Scar?" he mocks me.

"Can I please have some water?" I ask, in the most helpless voice I can muster.

I can sense his hesitation. "I'm gonna pass out. Water. Please."

I can practically hear his face contort into a scowl. There's already a glass sitting on the bathroom counter, which he fills with water and brings over to me. Two feet away. One. As he's holding out the glass, I take the only window of opportunity I've got and pick up the heavy cistern lid, swinging it with every bit of strength in my body. It isn't much, but it's enough, and he's taken completely by surprise as the porcelain smashes into his temple, sending him careening to the side, the glass of water flying through the air before smashing on the tiles between us.

I eye the length of rope in the bedroom, beyond the open bathroom door, as a devious plan begins to reveal itself in my drug-starved brain. Yes. Of course. I'll give him a taste of his own medicine, and maybe, just maybe, he'll give me back my medicine so I can breathe properly again.

I wonder briefly about the girl I helped, probably huddled in my apartment right now, waiting to be found. Or maybe she's already been found. Fucked if I know.

I don't really care, either. A good Samaritan act has turned into a fucking nightmare, and although it's taken me this long to get my shit together and move past the detachment and shock to start fighting for myself, I'm pretty fucking pleased with my efforts to knock Sal out. A thin trail of blood leads from his temple down into his mussed-up hair, the violent reality of his wound oddly satisfying.

I drag him into his bedroom. Fucker's heavy. I prop him up and tie his hands behind his back, securing them tightly to one of the bed posts. I collect the gun from his waistband, the car keys and phone from his pocket. I take his ridiculous driver's cap and put it on my own head, because *I'm* steering this motherfucking show right now.

When I'm convinced he's not going anywhere, I make my way downstairs to the kitchen, the gun gripped furiously tight in my sweat-slicked palm.

I'm getting myself a motherfucking drink if it's the last thing I do, and then I'm getting the fuck out of this house.

Fifteen minutes later, I'm nursing a glass of bourbon and waiting for Sal to wake up. He's taking his sweet time, so I eventually just tip a glass of water over his head. He comes to almost immediately, coughing and spluttering. I give him a big ol' *Fuck You* grin, taking a sip of bourbon that tastes pretty goddamn satisfying right now.

"Nice hat," he grumbles. "I'll make sure I bury you wearing it."

"Now, come on, Sal," I say. "I know it hurts, getting your ass handed to you by a girl, but don't worry. I won't tell anyone."

"Oh, yeah?" he says. "I've never heard that one before."

"I mean it," I say, taking another gulp of my drink and delighting in the way it burns as it slides down my throat. "Just tell me how to unlock your front door, and I'll be out of your hair."

See, I've spent the last fifteen minutes trying to get out of this fucking place. And I can't. Every door, every window, has this same fucking keypad stuck to it. The windows don't open. And the elevator door we came in from the basement is the same—it only works if you know the code.

Sal's eyes light up. "She set the alarm," he says, grinning. "That dumb bitch finally listened."

"Good for you," I say, feeling slightly uneasy at the fact that blonde playboy bunny could get herself out of this house, but I can't. It's infuriating.

"Here's the thing," Sal says. "I'm not giving you the alarm code, unless you tell me where Kaitlin is."

I pull the gun from my apron pocket and point it at him.

"Here's the thing," I say, mimicking his tone. "You're telling me exactly how to unlock that door, asshole, or I'll redecorate this room with your fucking brain matter."

CHAPTER TWELVE
ZETH

A PINEAPPLE SITS ON THE KITCHEN COUNTER. A *pineapple*. It's just not something you see everyday. It wasn't there when I went to bed last night, that's for sure. I'm all for eating fruit—you don't get a body like mine by shoving Twinkies down your throat twenty-four seven—but this thing looks like it requires preparation. It's fucking spiky. I stand in the kitchen, staring at it for a while, contemplating how to proceed, and then I figure, *fuck it, I'll wing it* and go on a mission to find a knife.

Sloane's still asleep upstairs in our bed. *Our* bed. I never thought I'd be thinking those words. It gives me insane pleasure to run a playback of what took place in that bed yesterday in minute detail as I carve up the fruit for my girl's breakfast. There was a lot of spanking involved. And a tiny clamp that I hooked up to Sloane's clit, firing electrical charges into her sweet pussy that had her clawing at my skin and screaming out my name. I fucking love when she does that.

It's one of those rare sunny mornings in Seattle. Like a damn finger of fate pointing straight down from Heaven, a pillar of light is shining straight through the glass doors at the front of the house, landing directly on the drawer where I stowed a small, velvet covered box three nights ago. A gift for Sloane. A gift I'm not ready to give her yet. Seems as though every time I walk past that goddamn drawer, I can feel the box inside humming like a freaking signalling beacon. I really need to move it. Take it down to the gym or something. Leave it in my locker there. She'd never find it amongst all my sweat-soaked work out clothes, hand wraps and boxing gloves. But then, no. That just seems fucking wrong.

I carry the sliced pineapple upstairs on a plate, along with the eggs I've made and some fresh orange juice. Very fucking domesticated. I would never have done this for anyone else. The stars would have collided and the universe collapsed in on itself before I bowed and scraped to any other chick. I don't see taking care of my girl as bowing and scraping now, though. I see it as making sure she's fed. Making sure she's content. Making sure she's safe. Making sure she's fit and healthy enough for me to fuck her the way I like, and for her to demand more.

She's still asleep when I enter the bedroom. Her dark hair is spilled across her pillow in loose waves around her head, her almost black eyelashes like charcoal smudges against her pale cheeks. She looks like she's been drawn or something.

Created out of thin air. I find myself thinking that a lot—that someone has crafted her, this mythical creature who's turned my life upside down—because how else can she be real? It makes no sense. The universe just isn't this kind to anyone, especially guys like me.

Placing the food down on the bedside table, I move up the bed, pulling the covers back from her body as I climb. She's naked underneath—so fucking perfect. Her breasts lay heavy, crushed between her arms as she lies on her side. I can already feel my cock stirring in my shorts. Nothing new there. Poor Sloane's eggs are going to be cold by the time she gets around to eating them. I haven't even made any food for myself. I knew *she* was all I was going to want to eat. Placing my hand on her hip, I gently turn her body so that she's on her back. Unlike my cock, her perfect nipples aren't erect yet, but I have plans on changing that. Slowly, carefully, I lower my mouth to her skin and I lick across her collarbone, moving down until I trace my tongue across the swell of her tits. So. Fucking. Amazing.

Sloane groans, body writhing a little as she surfaces into consciousness. Waking her up this way is the best goddamn part of my day. I know she's aware of what I'm doing when I feel her legs press together underneath me. She's been so good recently whenever we fuck, doing as I tell her when I tell her to without hesitation or question, that now I feel like being bad for her. She's earned it. I bite down on the now hard, tight bud of her nipple, sending a jolt of pain through her, waking her up properly. She reacts quickly, sucking in a sharp breath, her body tightening underneath me.

"Morning, Angry Girl. Dreaming about me?" I whisper.

Her fingers wind into my hair, which is longer than it's ever been. Not hipster long. Just long enough that she can get a good fucking handful of it and pull when she wants to. She moans, which is a good sign. There aren't many women you could wake up after a twelve hour hospital shift with a bite to the nipple and have them appreciate it. This is why we're fucking perfect together.

"You planning on backing that up?" she mumbles.

"What? This?" I bite her again, this time on the other nipple. Her eyelids fly open wide, her back arching off the bed. "Stay still, Angry Girl. Don't you dare fucking move unless I tell you to. If you're good, I'll make you come. Would you like that?"

"Yes," she says breathlessly. "I'd like that very much."

I hold myself over her, lowering myself a little more so that I can speak directly into her ear. "Okay. Spread your legs for me, Sloane," I growl. She shivers in that way she does. The way that lets me know she likes the sound of my voice, rough and right up close in her ear like that. She likes feeling my breath on her skin. Like the good fucking girl she is, she widens her legs for me, and I change positions, moving so I'm inside her legs now. My dick is so hard I'm pretty sure you could break rocks with it. I catch sight of her pussy and my balls begin to ache like they haven't been emptied in months, instead of yesterday morning.

Fuck.

"You're so fucking perfect," I groan. "God. Your pussy is beautiful. So pink. So sweet." I can smell her, that peculiar yet addicting scent that drives me absolutely crazy. I just want to bury my face between her legs and go to town. Not yet, though. "You want me to make you wet, Angry Girl?" I ask.

Sloane looks up at me with those big brown eyes of hers and nods. "I'm already wet," she whispers. She used to sound ashamed of the fact when she admitted that to me, but not anymore. She knows how much it turns me on to see her dripping wet and ready for me. As if to prove the point, she rocks her hips upward, giving me a better view.

"You're breaking the rules," I inform her. "I didn't say you could move." Palming her right breast, I squeeze hard, tightrope walking that boundary between enjoyable pain and real discomfort. Sloane's hips press back down into the mattress in an instant, her eyes closing as she breathes through what I'm doing to her. "That's better. Yeah. Good girl..." I let my other hand trail down the side of her body, my fingers slowly working toward the apex of her thighs. I don't go straight for her clit, though. I run my fingers up the insides of the legs, over her hips, up her stomach, breasts, neck, over her high cheekbones and over her lips.

"Suck," I tell her.

She obeys, opening her mouth, allowing me to slide my fingers inside. Her mouth is hot and wet, and has my cock throbbing so hard. She's so good at blowing me now. She had no clue what she was doing the very first time back in that darkened hotel room, but her inexperience and her tight mouth had almost been enough to make me come on the spot. Now that she knows what she's doing with that tongue of hers, she has the power to rob me of all fucking common sense.

She grazes her teeth against my knuckles and I can imagine all too well what that would feel like if it were my cock in her mouth. I can't help but hiss as she sucks harder. "You're being so good," I whisper into her hair. I let go of her breast and prop myself up on one elbow so I can slide my fingers from her mouth and place them between her legs, wetting her with her own saliva.

"Fuck, Zeth." Her head kicks back, rocking to one side as I work my fingertips in small, tight, purposeful circles over her clit. She's staring at me, beautiful, so turned on I can see it in her eyes, when I lift my fingers to my own mouth and slide them inside. She tastes so fucking good. Guys say that about girls all the time, but I really fucking mean it. The taste of her pussy on my tongue is enough to send the blood roaring through my veins like combustion fuel in a high-powered engine. I feel like I could do zero to a hundred in less than a second.

"Fuck, Sloane. You're incredible. Lift your knees for me. *Now.*" She bridges her legs, feet pressed flat against the bed, and holds them there. I know she wants to let her knees fall to the sides, opening herself up for me, but she's good. She waits.

That clamp from yesterday enters my head, stowed safely back in the black duffel I keep in the bottom of the wardrobe, but I reject that idea. I do want to make her moan. I do want to make her twitch. But I want my head between her legs, too, and I can't lick her with that thing in the way.

My eyes catch on the plate I brought up here with me and

I know what I'm going to do. Reaching over, I pick up a piece of the pineapple and throw it into my mouth. Tastes so sweet it twinges at the sides of my tongue. "Mmm, yeah, baby. You're gonna like this, and so am I," I say. Sloane fights back a surprised smile as I take another piece of the pineapple and I head down between her legs.

I'm not in the mood to be careful. Fuck that. Shoving her knees apart myself, I get down there and take hold of her ankles, throwing her legs over my shoulders. "Are you ready, Angry Girl?"

She bites her lip, her head rolling back. I know she wants to arch her back off the bed again, lift her hips up to meet my mouth, but she knows there'll be consequences if she does. I'll tease the fuck out of her for hours and I won't let her come, and that's not something she enjoys. Me, on the other hand... Torturing her like that gives me a particular thrill that no amount of breakfast making and domesticated life will be able to tamp down.

I bite carefully down on the piece of cold pineapple and press it into her pussy with my mouth. She gasps, hands tightening as I work it up and down, slowly tracing it from the entrance to her pussy all the way up to her clit. I want to pump my fingers inside her. I want to make her fucking scream. I can be patient when the situation calls for it, though. Instead I tease her with the piece of fruit, enjoying the flavor of it mixed in with the slick juices of her tight, amazing pussy.

I can't help myself. I have to touch myself. Reaching down, I slide my hand inside my boxers and I take hold of my cock, squeezing the tip. Feels fucking amazing, but I know sinking myself balls deep into the woman in this bed is going to be a million times better. I'm already planning where I'm going to come. Over her tits. In her mouth. Her stomach. Her back. I want to mark her all over with my come, rub it into her skin. Into her pussy. Claim her as mine.

I swallow the pineapple, and then I set to working my tongue over Sloane's clit. The fruit was fun, but I don't need it anymore. I just need her pussy in my mouth and her come on my tongue. And I'm gonna make it fucking happen right now. Carefully, I push my index finger inside her, teasing myself as much as her with how slowly I do it. She's trembling violently by the time I'm knuckle-deep. She's so tight. I'll never get over how incredible her body is. How tightly she squeezes my cock when I'm inside her.

I can't wait to get to that point. First, I let myself pump her with my fingers, knowing she's imagining they're my cock. I go slow at first but then pick up speed, matching the motion with the sweeps of my tongue over her swollen clit. I could suck on the hot bundle of nerves and make her explode, I know I could. But I refrain. This is just too much fucking fun.

She's begging me to let her come by the time I give in. And she really does fucking explode. I lick and suck at her, groaning like a goddamn savage as she comes all over my tongue. So. Fucking. Hot. She buries her hands in my hair and grinds up against me, her body shaking, falling apart as she climaxes.

I have absolutely no self-control after that. As soon as the tension falls out of her body, her muscles sinking heavy into the mattress, I grab hold of her hips and spin her over, throwing her onto her front and then lifting her hips so that her ass is in the air. "We're not done yet, Angry Girl." I lay my hand against her skin, making a sharp cracking sound as my palm connects with the soft curve of her ass.

"Fuck!" She gasps out, instinctively grabbing hold of the bed sheets, like she knows how hard I'm about to fuck her. Like she knows she's about to be seeing stars. I lose the boxers, and then there's nothing between me and my angry girl. I trace my cock from her clit upward, gauging her reaction, seeing where she wants me to stop...where she wants me the most. I don't even make it to her ass. She's pushing back against me, panting hard as I tease the tip of my dick against the opening of her pussy.

"You want me, Sloane? How bad do you want me inside you right now?"

"Fuck. Please. Please... Please... I need you," she moans.

I could wait, I could play with her some more, but my balls feel like they're going to burst. I slam myself home, not holding back, fire singing through my veins as Sloane screams out my name.

My fingers dig into her hips as I pull her back against me. She doesn't resist. She moves with me, sighing and melting against me as I thrust so hard I'm seeing stars myself. When we come, we come together, and we're both incoherent.

Just. Too. Good.

We collapse together onto the bed as one, me still inside her, my body angled slightly to the side to keep my weight off her. When we've both regained our breath, I begin tracing my fingers absentmindedly up and down her side. Her skin is soft as silk. "You bought weird fruit," I whisper into her hair.

She laughs, and the feel of it travels through her and into me, spreading some deep, strange contentment down into my bones. This woman is going to be the end of me. "I did it for you," she says.

"Oh? How d'you figure that?"

"They say..." She seems bemused. "They say that if you eat lots of pineapple, it makes you taste good."

The irony of what she's said hits me full on, given that I've just used a piece of it between her legs. I bite down lightly on her shoulder, growling. "You don't need to eat anything to taste good, Sloane. I'm addicted to how you taste, just as you are."

She laughs. "Well, since you spend about ninety per cent of your day with your head between my legs, I just wanted to make sure you enjo—" The sound of my burner ringing on the bedside table cuts her off. We both just look at it. Before earlier this morning when the Barbieri brothers called me, the thing hasn't rung in...in fucking forever. Since shit went down with my ex-employer and everything changed. And now it's ringing again? Bets are on it being Theo again. I do *not* want to talk to him. I don't want to talk to anyone who might be asking me to beat the ever loving shit out of anyone, or worse. It's not as though I've gone soft. I'll still tear anyone limb from limb should the situation require it, but it's more on an as needed basis. For protection and defense as apposed to for money.

Sloane presses her face into the pillow, and a muffled,

"You'd better get that," reaches my ears. I do answer, but only because the people who are likely to call my burner aren't the kind of people who give up after calling once.

When I hear the voice on the other end of the line, I find that the Barbieri situation has been escalated up the ranks. "Zeth," Roberto Barbieri, the Barber of Brooklyn himself, says. "I hear you didn't much like talking to my sons?"

"I'm more of an email kind of guy these days."

"Good to know. I'll make sure to forward you the details of our arrangement in a message once our conversation is over, then. Does that suit you?"

"And what arrangement might that be? I already told Theo, I'm not working for anyone else anymore." I don't like this guy's tone of voice. I sure as fuck don't like how he's ruining my post orgasm glow. Sloane's watching me with wide eyes, clearly able to hear what's being said. There's a time not too long ago when I would have left the room, but not anymore. I don't hide anything from her these days. She knows all about the fights, the underground gambling, and the occasional gun deal that goes down at the fighting gym I run. She knows me, knows who I am, and knows I will never live on the straight and narrow like other, normal people. She can handle fights and dirty money so long as I'm not getting hurt. And she can handle the guns so long as I don't get my ass shot.

I doubt very much she'd handle me going out on task for the Barber of Brooklyn, though.

"Zeth, you and I both know this sedentary life you're leading isn't what you were built for. You're a cutthroat, just like I am. I'm coming for Seattle. You must have known someone would eventually. I'm laying out my cards here and now. New York is where the throne of my empire rests. I can't be in two places at once. I need someone to run my west coast operations, and I want that someone to be you."

"I have no interest in being your understudy, Roberto. Absolutely no fucking interest whatsoever." The guy is crazy if he thinks I'm putting myself into yet another position like I was in with Charlie. You don't climb out from underneath the shit heap only to voluntarily climb back under again.

"I can understand your reluctance, Zeth, I really can. But you are a very dangerous individual. If I place someone else in charge over there, I wouldn't be able to allow a man like you to be operating in the same district. It wouldn't be smart business."

"I'm not operating. I run a few fights and broker a few deals. You don't need to concern yourself with what I'm doing, Roberto. I'm none of your fucking business."

"And what about the lovely young Ms. Romera? Will she end up being my business? I fear she will if we can't find a way to make both of us happy right now."

Sloane sits up, clearly having heard her name. She looks mildly concerned, which makes my blood boil. Who does this guy think he fucking is, threatening her to get his own way? I won't allow it. I will burn down his whole fucking New York empire before I let that happen. "You don't say her name. You don't *ever* say her name," I growl.

"Don't forget who you're talking to right now, boy. I'm bigger and I'm badder than Charlie Holsan ever was. When I offer someone a title within my organization, they fucking jump," he spits. "And this isn't just any old title. I'm offering to make you the motherfucking King of the west coast. You'd be answerable to no one but me. You need to think about this for a couple of hours, Zeth. Bear in mind, I don't make these kinds of calls personally very often. It's unlikely I'll be making another one. And also, you should bear in mind that I am *not* someone to be fucked with."

I laugh, and it feels raw in my throat. Caustic, poisonous laughter that gives away what I think of his threats before I can put my thoughts into words. "I vowed after Charlie that I would never be answerable to anyone ever again. And I won't. I don't want to be the King of the west coast or anywhere else for that matter. And something *you* should bear in mind, Roberto? I *am* a dangerous individual. And people don't usually live to tell the tale after fucking with *me* either."

CHAPTER THIRTEEN
GRACIE

SERVING IN THE MILITARY TEACHES YOU A LOT ABOUT ... well, everything. My time in the army taught me how to overcome fear and think with a cool head in situations where I might otherwise break down. It taught me how to fight, how to defend myself and those around me. It also taught me how to deal with hostage situations.

And *this* was not what I was taught. Allowing myself to get side tracked by Theo Barbieri administering a very particular brand of punishment to an apparently dim-witted blonde is not how I should be passing the time. I should have fucking bolted. I mean, come on, Gracie? What the fuck?

My cell phone is gone. It's around about now that my employer will be flipping his shit. He's used to me picking up whenever he calls, and the fact that I was escorting up his precious, spoiled-ass daughter today means he will have phoned the moment it looked like we were waylaid. He's going to be furious. He wanted me to bring Ian with me— *two men on the job are always better than one, love*—but I'd told him I could handle a simple pick-up. It hadn't escaped my attention that he'd said two *men*. He's always been like that—unwilling to believe I can be good at my job. When my parents died and Paddy took me in, he told me that being strong had nothing to do with your sex. It had everything to do with determination and willingness to sacrifice. If I was willing to sacrifice the love I felt for my parents, it wouldn't hurt that they were gone anymore. That was being strong. If I was willing to sacrifice petty things like boys and shopping and high heels, if I concentrated and trained hard, I could become the kind of person other people feared. That's always been a big thing for Paddy: instilling fear in others. So I did whatever he told me to. I stopped loving my dead parents and I didn't kiss boys, and the people of the McLaughlin household hug the motherfucking wall when I walk by them, but still ... Paddy's never believed I'm cut-throat enough to survive his world. I've always felt like a disappointment to him. *Always.* It's his own daughter who should be the disappointment, and yet the girl can do no wrong. She fucks around. She takes drugs. She has a foul temper on her and is constantly finding herself in situations that would get most people killed, and yet the old man thinks the sun shines out of her perfect little ass. I mean, she's the reason behind the entire feud between the Barbieris and the McLaughlins, after all. Waiting in the musty-smelling dry store with nothing to do but kill time, I find myself wondering if Theo knows about that.

He's gone for an hour. When he comes back, I'm ready for him. I've smashed a jar from one of the shelves and I'm hiding behind the door like a goddamn idiot with a shard of glass in my hand. I'm a second away from sinking the wicked point into his neck when I see he's already bleeding. That kind of throws me.

Theo looks at me, looks at the weapon in my hand and then has the gall to look unimpressed. "Planning on slitting my throat?"

"Thinking about it."

"Awesome. Make sure you dig in deep. My father only just about broke the skin."

"I didn't think Roberto Barbieri went half-assed on Columbian neckties."

Theo gives me a bland smile. "Turns out being his son does have its occasional advantages. Now, you gonna shank me with that, or are we gonna get the hell out of here before we both end up dead?"

"You letting me go?"

He quirks one eyebrow upward, clearly amused by the thought. "When you've helped me figure out where Kaitlin is, I'll be glad to part company with you."

"And how the hell do you think I'll be able to do that? She ran, remember. New York's a big place, in case you hadn't noticed. I'm not psychic. I can't just concentrate really hard and somehow know exactly where she is."

"True. But what about if you had this?" He reaches into his pocket and pulls out a cell phone—*mine*. The screen's shattered but it's lit up. Chances are it's still working.

"You took that from the car."

"I did. And when we get to my place, you're going to call your ward and find out where the hell she is. And then we're going to find my brother and go get this girl, and then you can be on your merry way."

He's dreaming if he thinks I'm actually going to do that for him, but I flash him a cold smile anyway. "Sure. If you can get me out of here, that is." I'd have made a break for it already if I weren't convinced that I'd end up with my head mounted on one of the Barber of Brooklyn's living room walls. I'm just one person, and, yeah, I can fight, but Cucina Diavolo is massive and full of guys who can also fight. I don't have a death wish, so I've done the smart thing and stayed put. Theo knows this place, though. He knows how to sneak me out. If he thinks I'll help him find Kaitlin, he'll take me back to his place, wherever that is, and I can slip him there, no problem.

Theo watches me, green eyes skimming over each of my facial features in turn, as though he's trying to figure me out. Or maybe it's because of what he did to that blonde and how badly he made me squirm. I hate that he saw that. "Turn around," he says.

"Why?"

Holding up a pair of handcuffs, he grins at me. "I'd say I'm not going to enjoy this, but I'd be lying."

Kind of ridiculous that he thinks I can't work my way out of a pair of handcuffs, but whatever. I toss the shard of glass onto the ground and turn around, holding my wrists together behind my back. If he really does think I won't jimmy my way out of the cuffs, perhaps that will make him even more complacent. I might be able to grab my phone and get the hell out of Dodge before we even get to his place.

"Being such a good girl," he says. His breath hits the back of my neck, warm and close. My body reacts automatically, against my will, making the skin across my shoulders break out in goose bumps. It's fucked that he's having an effect on me whatsoever. I seriously do not like it. Why couldn't he have been disfigured or something, instead of some smoking-hot Italian god with green eyes? Fate is a cruel bitch.

I shiver as I feel the cold press of the metal snapping closed around my wrists. Theo must have cuffed a lot of people in the past; he tightens them enough so that they're digging into my skin, giving me no room to contort my hands and slide them free. It doesn't matter, though. There's more than one way to get myself free.

The next few minutes are adrenaline filled as I'm led silently out of the pokey room and down the corridor. We descend the stairs at the end of the hallway but instead of turning right and heading back through the kitchen, Theo guides me to the left, along another hallway. I can hear someone shouting—angry threats about cutting off someone's balls. By the stern, cold look on Theo's face I know it's his father. Has to be. My suspicions are confirmed when I hear the infuriated voice hissing, "This isn't just any old title. I'm offering to make you the motherfucking King of the west coast. You'd be answerable to no one but me. You—"

Theo hurries me along through more winding hallways, preventing me from hearing the rest of the conversation, his hand resting in the small of my back. He looks troubled. We pass a waitress, not the blonde from earlier but another one, dark hair pulled back into a perfect chignon. She looks Italian, like she could be Theo's sister or something. But she's not. I know enough about the Barbieri family to know Theo and Salvatore were the Barber's only children. The waitress smiles politely at Theo, dark brown eyes skimming over me as though she doesn't even see me. I'm hardly surprised. Paddy's employees are just as discreet.

We end up walking straight through the floor of the restaurant, more waiters and waitresses acknowledging Theo and pointedly ignoring me, and then we're out on the streets of Hell's Kitchen. A sleek black 1969 Ford Mustang idles at the roadside, a tall, chubby guy in a neatly pressed suit leaning against the driver side door. He straightens when he sees Theo, hands folded in front of him. Theo walks with me around the other side of the car, unfazed by the people on the sidewalk; he presses his body up close behind mine, so close that people would assume we were lovers and not that he was trying to conceal my handcuffed wrists. I'm bundled into the car and then Theo is talking to the chubby guy. It almost makes me laugh when I hear him telling the guy off for leaning against the Mustang. I mean, the guy's priorities must be fucked if he's worried about his paintwork right now. When he climbs into the car, he's wearing a grim expression.

"It's not exactly comfortable trying to sit like this with my arms pinned behind my back. You feel like taking these off me now?"

"No."

Well, shit. It was worth a shot. Theo guns the engine and merges into the slow-moving traffic, eyes fixed steadily in the rearview mirror. He's tense. Even more tense than he was before, inside the building. By the way he's paying more attention to what's happening behind us instead of what's going on in front, I'd say he thinks we're being followed. I casually glance in the side mirror, seeing if I can spot anything. I get the idea into my head that Paddy might already have someone watching the Barbieris' place, but that's just wishful thinking. After about fifteen minutes, I'm pretty sure we're not being tailed and it would seem so is Theo. He relaxes, tapping his fingers against the steering wheel. I decide to fuck with him. If he won't take the handcuffs off, then why the hell should I behave myself? I kick my foot up, resting it against the dash, the heel of my boot making a scraping sound as I drag it across the console.

Theo's eyes go wide. Gripping hold of the steering wheel, he stares at my foot on the dash, unblinking and unmoving. I'm fairly certain he's stopped breathing. "What do you think you're doing?" he asks.

"Trying to make the best out of a bad situation."

"Get your feet down. Now."

"Or what? Are you gonna kick me out of the car?" One can always dream.

"No. But I will shoot you in the thigh. Jesus, woman, you're scuffing everything!"

I am, as well. It gives me great pleasure to see the long mark I leave behind when I let my foot fall back into the foot well. Theo swears the whole way across Hell's Kitchen and into Tribeca, where he takes us along the wharf and parks the Mustang outside a low, sprawling warehouse. The place has been restored, converted into living space. The tinted windows and the lack of dirt really give away its residential status. I try not to look impressed as Theo hustles me out of the car and inside the place.

The warehouse is one large, open-plan space inside. Haphazardly placed furniture splits the floor into different areas—a monstrous black leather couch separates the living-room area from the sleeping area, where a huge king-sized bed sits against the back wall. The kitchen runs down the side of one wall. No bathroom in sight. That must be tucked away through the only other door I can see, positioned in between a row of bookcases.

I'm not interested in how the guy's decorated, or what books he's been reading. I'm only interested in an escape route, and it appears that there's only one: back the way we just came in. The windows are too high to climb out of, and there are no other exits that I can see.

"Sit down," Theo commands. He nudges me toward the couch, so I sink myself down on it, throwing my feet up again. The only reaction I get out of him is raised eyebrows. Seems he's not as precious about his couch as he is about his car. "Now. You're gonna phone Kaitlin and you're gonna find out where she is. And then all of this will be over."

I know it won't be over. Does he really think I'm that gullible? "Do you care if McLaughlin knows you're the one responsible for kidnapping his daughter?" I ask.

"It wouldn't be ideal."

144

"Then why do you expect me to believe I'll be walking free as soon as you have Kaitlin in your possession? You know I'll tell Paddy you took her on your father's orders. There'd be a hell of a lot of Italian blood running through the streets of the Kitchen."

"And Irish blood, too," he replies. "My father won't care, so long as we do what we set out to do. He'll go to war with Paddy over this. It doesn't matter to him."

"And what does matter to him?"

"Justice." For a second I think Theo does know about what Kaitlin did all those years ago, but then he says something else that changes my mind. "Paddy screwed my cousin, Sara. The woman we passed on the way out of the restaurant? He fucked her to piss off my father. Roberto isn't the kind of guy who would let that slide without sending a message."

"So Roberto wants a seventeen-year-old girl to pay the price for her father's mistakes."

Theo just stares at me, a small frown creasing his forehead. He's not going to argue with me about it, that much is clear. After a moment he pulls my smashed cell phone from his pocket again and holds it up for me to see. "What's the code, Gracie?"

"Hand it over and I'll put it in for you."

"I don't think so."

"Then I can't remember the code."

"You have three texts here from McLaughlin. Tell me the code and I'll read them to you."

I growl under my breath, pulling at the cuffs. I can't believe the bastard is blackmailing me with text messages that

I'm sure he wants to read just as badly as I do. I really do want to know what the old man is saying, though. He could be telling me he already has Kaitlin and that he's coming to find me next. He could be worried about me.

"All right. Fine. It's one zero nine one."

Theo pulls a face as he types the numbers into the cracked glass. He looks pleasantly surprised when the phone opens for him, as though he expected me to be lying.

"Read them to me. What's he saying?" I snap.

Theo flicks to the messages and reads, his face a mask of concentration and then mild amusement as he checks what Paddy sent to me. "Oh, dear. Looks like someone's in trouble," he says.

A lead weight sinks in my gut. "Show me, asshole."

He ignores the aggression in my voice and stands in front of me, obliging me by turning the phone to face me. The first message isn't so bad.

> ETA? The boys say the flight came in on time.

The time stamp on the second text is an hour later, and the tone is a hell of a lot more pissed off.

> Gracie, where the fuck is my daughter? If something's happened, you'd better fucking tell me right now. My daughter better be fucking safe.

And then:

146

> If you're reading this and you have my daughter, return her safely to me and I'll kill you quickly. If you're reading this and you have the woman supposed to be protecting Kaitlin, do me a favor and put a bullet in between her fucking eyes.

"Doesn't seem too happy with you, huh?" Theo says, smiling. "I wonder what happened to the whole *he thinks of me as his blood* bit. Correct me if I'm wrong but didn't he just green light your execution? Seems to be Old Man McLaughlin definitely prefers his daughter over you any day of the week."

Bile burns in the back of my throat. Not ten seconds ago I was actually stupid enough to be thinking that maybe Paddy would be worried about me. I should have known better, though. I'm a means to an end. It's all I've ever been. And now that I've failed him, now that I've lost his daughter, I'm utterly expendable. Fucking bastard.

"I'm going to uncuff you," Theo says.

This is surprising, though not unwelcome. The blood flow to my hands feels like it was cut off about twenty minutes ago. "Why would you do that?"

"Because you're going to make that phone call for me now, aren't you?" He looks deadly serious, a dash of curiosity on his handsome face. "You can't go back to McLaughlin. You have no reason to care about the girl now, right? And from the murderous expression on your face, I'm guessing you're pretty pissed off at the Irish. The guy just ordered you dead. If you know a better way to get back at him than taking something he loves from him, then please ... enlighten me."

I swallow down the fury rising in my throat, fighting to keep myself from screaming. This is one messed-up situation. This morning I thought I was going to be babysitting Kaitlin for the next three weeks, bored out of my head but glad of the opportunity to prove myself to Paddy. And now it looks like I can't even go home. Theo's right. I am mad. I'm furious. I slide my hands underneath my butt, working them forward until I can bend my body and step through the loop my joined wrists make. Holding my wrists up for him to free me, I make my decision.

"Okay. I'll make the call. I'll help you. But you have to promise me one thing."

"Which is?"

"You have to promise you're going to kill her. You have to promise you'll kill Kaitlin."

HART
SAINT
GERMAIN

ABOUT THE AUTHORS

LILI SAINT GERMAIN

Lili writes dark, disturbing romance. Her USA Today and #1 iBooks Bestselling GYPSY BROTHERS SERIES focuses on a morally bankrupt biker gang and the girl who seeks her vengeance upon them. The USA Today and #1 iBooks bestselling CARTEL SERIES is a prequel trilogy of full-length novels that explores the beginnings of the club, published worldwide in print and ebook by HarperCollins. Lili's Gypsy Brothers books have sold over half a million copies worldwide.

Lili quit corporate life to focus on writing and so far is loving every minute of it. Her other loves in life include her gorgeous husband and beautiful daughter, good coffee, Tarantino movies and spending hours on Pinterest.

You can get book #1 in the GYPSY BROTHERS SERIES FREE on all platforms HERE:
www.lilisaintgermain.com/books/seven-sons/

If you want to get an automatic email when Lili's next book is released, sign up at http://eepurl.com/beYVNr. Your email address will never be shared and you can unsubscribe at any time.

FOR HELL'S KITCHEN SERIES UPDATES

sign up at
http://eepurl.com/beYVNr

LILI ALWAYS LOVES HEARING FROM READERS.

You can find her in the following places:

Facebook Page:
https://www.facebook.com/pages/Lili-Saint-
Germain/225567900945786

Facebook profile:
https://www.facebook.com/lili.saintgermain.18

Twitter: https://twitter.com/LiliStGermain1

Lili's Website: http://www.lilisaintgermain.com

Instagram: https://instagram.com/lili_stgermain/

Email: lilisaintgermain@gmail.com

CALLIE HART

Callie Hart is a bagel eating, coffee drinking, romance addict. She can recite lines from the Notebook by heart. She lives on a ridiculously high floor in a way-too expensive building with her fiancé and their pet goldfish, Neptune. Her internationally bestselling **BLOOD & ROSES SERIES** has garnered over 1000 5* reviews, and caused mass swooning sessions the world over.

You can read book one, **DEVIANT**, for FREE
by heading HERE:
http://calliehart.com/deviant

If you want to know the second one of Callie's books goes live, all you need to do is sign up at http://eepurl.com/IzhzL.

IN THE MEANTIME, CALLIE WANTS
TO HEAR FROM YOU!

Callie's website: http://calliehart.com

Facebook Page:
http://www.facebook.com/calliehartauthor

Facebook Profile:
http://www.facebook.com/callie.hart.777

Blog: http://calliehart.blogspot.com.au

Twitter: http://www.twitter.com/_callie_hart

Goodreads: http://www.goodreads.com/author/
show/7771953.Callie_Hart

To sign up for her newsletter, head to
http://eepurl.com/IzhzL.

FOR HELL'S KITCHEN SERIES UPDATES

sign up at
http://eepurl.com/beYVNr

HART
SAINT
GERMAIN

ADDITIONAL WORKS

BLOOD & ROSES SERIES

Deviant (FREE)
Fracture
Burn
Fallen
Twisted
Collateral

DEAD MAN'S INK SERIES

Rebel

THE GYPSY BROTHERS SERIES

Seven Sons (FREE)
Six Brothers
Five Miles
Four Score
Three Years
Two Roads
One Love

THE CARTEL TRILOGY

Cartel

44622740R00089

Made in the USA
Lexington, KY
04 September 2015